MYTHOLOGY
AROUND
THE WORLD

# GODS
AND
HEROES

KORWIN BRIGGS

WORKMAN PUBLISHING ★ NEW YORK

LIBRARY OF CONGRESS CATALOGING-IN-PUBLICATION DATA IS AVAILABLE.

ISBN 978-1-5235-0378-0

WORKMAN BOOKS ARE AVAILABLE AT SPECIAL DISCOUNTS WHEN PURCHASED
IN BULK FOR PREMIUMS AND SALES PROMOTIONS AS WELL AS FOR FUND-RAISING
OR EDUCATIONAL USE. SPECIAL EDITIONS OR BOOK EXCERPTS CAN ALSO BE CREATED
TO SPECIFICATION. FOR DETAILS, CONTACT THE SPECIAL SALES DIRECTOR AT
THE ADDRESS BELOW, OR SEND AN EMAIL TO SPECIALMARKETS@WORKMAN.COM.

WORKMAN PUBLISHING CO., INC.
225 VARICK STREET
NEW YORK, NY 10014
WORKMAN.COM

WORKMAN IS A REGISTERED TRADEMARK OF WORKMAN PUBLISHING CO., INC.

PRINTED IN CHINA

FIRST PRINTING JULY 2018

10 9 8 7 6 5 4 3 2 1

# CONTENTS

# INTRODUCTION

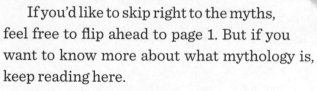

**W**elcome to *Gods and Heroes*! You hold in your hands hundreds of myths and stories from across history and around the world. Inside this book you'll find earthshaking battles, daring adventures, loves gained, lost, and kidnapped, great gods, fearsome monsters, the world's heaviest cat, and the truth about Medusa (spoiler: It's sad).

If you'd like to skip right to the myths, feel free to flip ahead to page 1. But if you want to know more about what mythology is, keep reading here.

## WHAT ARE MYTHS?

Myths are the traditional stories of a culture. Some are sacred tales that teach people about their gods. Some explain the unexplainable, like how the world began and what happens when we die. Some tell the histories of peoples and nations. And some offer guidance on what's good, what's evil, and how to live.

## WHY DO MYTHS MATTER?

In myths, we can see reflections of the people who wrote them—what they thought of the world and themselves, how they were different from us, and how they were the same.

As you read the myths in this book, it might be helpful to keep this question in mind: Why might this culture have thought it was important to continue telling this tale, year after year, generation after generation? If you keep an open mind, you might learn something you didn't expect.

## WHERE DO MYTHS COME FROM?

No one knows who told the first myths, or when, or why. One timeworn theory says that myths were originally stories of actual historical events, made more magical by thousands of years of retellings, like a giant, ancient game of telephone. Others say myths started as answers to tough questions (What's the sun? It's a god!). Yet another theory claims that myths come from the deep, unconscious parts of our minds, which is why so many civilizations have similar stories of gods and monsters and floods and heroes, despite never having met each other.

As societies evolved, so did their myths. They changed with the times, the places, and the people telling them. Local myths mixed with foreign myths; tribal myths were retold as the myths of towns, cities, and countries. Some myths spread across entire continents, while others disappeared entirely.

## WHAT WE DON'T KNOW AND WHY WE DON'T KNOW IT

For most of human history, there was no such thing as writing. If you wanted to know about a legend, you had to listen to someone who could tell you about it. Some people dedicated their lives to memorizing hours and hours of stories, word for word, just to keep the tales alive. More often people would memorize what they thought was most important and fill in the rest as best they could. When the storyteller died, so did the myth (or at least, their version of it).

The result is that most of the world's myths are lost forever. All we have are the ones that someone happened to write down. And we can't always be sure about those, either. Just because something is written doesn't make it right. Sometimes people make mistakes, or make things up. When there are enough sources, we can compare what they have in common and tease out the truth, but often we have to do our best with just one or two.

## A DISCLAIMER

While this book tries to keep the tone light and upbeat, some of these myths contain violence and cruelty. If you run into any that offend you, it might help to remember that the original authors of these stories died centuries before anyone had ever heard of "PG."

# LEGEND

Throughout this book, you will see many different kinds of banners. Each banner represents a different culture.

**AMERICAN GREAT PLAINS**

**AUSTRALIAN**

**CELTIC**

**CENTRAL ASIAN**

**CHINESE**

**EAST AFRICAN**

**EGYPTIAN**

**GREEK/ROMAN**

**HAWAIIAN**

**INCAN**

**INDIAN/HINDU**

**INUIT**

**JAPANESE/SHINTO**

**MAORI**

**MESOAMERICAN**

**NORSE**

**NORTHWESTERN NORTH AMERICAN**

**PERSIAN**

**SEMITIC**

**SLAVIC**

**SOUTHWESTERN NORTH AMERICAN**

**SUMERIAN/ MESOPOTAMIAN**

**WEST AFRICAN**

At the top of each entry you will also see some information that tells you which mythological tradition each character comes from, where they are believed to live, and any aliases they might have.

## HERACLES

**TRADITION:** Greek/Roman
**HOME:** Mount Olympus
**ALSO KNOWN AS:** Hercules

Next to the information will be one of these three symbols, which indicate whether you are reading about a god, a hero, or a creature.

**GODS**

**HEROES**

**CREATURES**

# GLOSSARY

Before we begin, here are a few words worth knowing.

**ANIMISM:** The belief that creatures, plants, and other things have spirits.

**IMMORTALITY:** Eternal life; an immortal is someone (especially a god) who lives forever, while a mortal is someone who can die.

**MONOTHEISM:** A religion that has only one god.

**PAGANISM:** A religion that isn't one of the major world religions.

**PANTHEON:** A culture's group of gods (i.e., the Greek pantheon or the Norse pantheon).

**POLYTHEISM:** A religion that has more than one god.

# AMATERASU

## RADIANT SUN GODDESS

# AMATERASU

**TRADITION:** Japanese/Shinto
**HOME:** The High Celestial Plain
**ALSO KNOWN AS:** Amaterasu Ōmikami
(The Great Divinity Illuminating Heaven)

The leaders of most pantheons are gods, not goddesses. It's not fair, but it's true, and it's hardly the gods' fault. Mythologies reflect the societies that create them, and most societies whose myths we know about have been led by men. One major exception is Amaterasu, the highest goddess of Japan. Amaterasu is the spirit of the sun, the ruler of the realms of gods and people, and the original ancestor of the Japanese emperors. She is a beautiful, warm, radiant goddess who became even more powerful over a long and eventful life. Here are just a couple of her most famous myths.

## AMATERASU AND THE NEARLY ENDLESS NIGHT

Amaterasu stars in one of the most famous Shinto myths: the disappearance of Amaterasu.

Grieving and scared after her brother Susanoo destroyed her fields, threw a horse into her weaving area, killed her handmaiden, and pooped on her dining room floor (seriously), Amaterasu fled her home and hid in Heavenly Rock Cave. The thing is, Amaterasu was the sun goddess. When she left, so did the sun itself, plunging the world into cold and darkness. People couldn't see, plants couldn't grow, and natural disasters raged across the land and sea. Without the sun, the world faced destruction. Something had to be done.

Eight hundred gods assembled to bring Amaterasu back. But despite begging, pleading, and a half-baked plan involving songbirds, Amaterasu refused to leave her cave. So, the gods came up with a bigger, better, dancier plan.

They used their power to create a magic mirror and set it up in front of Amaterasu's cave. Then, they all began a chant while a beautiful goddess did a magical dance. The gods laughed and yelled and carried on as loudly as they could, until finally Amaterasu opened her cave door, just a crack, to see what was causing the commotion. The gods said they were celebrating, because at long last they had found a goddess even greater than Amaterasu. Amaterasu's gaze fell upon the mirror, and she mistook her reflection for this new goddess. When she leaned out farther for a better look, the gods grabbed hold of her, pulled her from the cave, and tied a magical rope across the entrance to prevent her from ever hiding there again. With Amaterasu back, the sun returned, and the world was saved.

If you believe the stories, the mirror that the gods used to trick Amaterasu out of her cave is still owned by the imperial family of Japan and is presented to each new Japanese emperor.

## HOW THE SUN CONQUERED JAPAN

At her birth, Amaterasu was granted rulership of the Celestial Plains, but not Earth. She won Earth through conquest, starting with Izumo, a small region of Japan ruled by a king named Okuninushi.

Before invading, she sent her son Ama-no-Hoki to explore the area, learn what he could, and report back to heaven on what he found. But almost as soon as he arrived, Ama-no-Hoki forgot what he was doing and settled down to live on Earth. After some time with no contact, Amaterasu sent Ama-no-Hoki's son after him.

A year went by, and then another. After three years without a message from either her son or grandson, Amaterasu sent another god, Ama-no-waka-hiko, to find out what had happened. But instead of searching for her son and grandson (who, it turned out, had also settled down), Ama-no-waka-hiko made friends with King Okuninushi, married his daughter, and (depending on who's telling the story) either forgot about his mission or decided to take the land for himself.

After eight more years without any contact, Amaterasu sent a divine pheasant to figure out what was going on. When Ama-no-waka-hiko saw it coming, he shot an arrow at it so fast that, after passing right through the bird, the arrow continued flying all the way up to heaven, where it landed at another god's feet. The other god picked it up and threw it back down—right into Ama-no-waka-hiko, killing him instantly.

Now, a full eleven years later, Amaterasu was no closer to ruling Izumo than when she started. This time she sent down two gods to negotiate with Okuninushi. They arrived before him in a show of power and grace, sitting cross-legged on the tips of their swords while riding a tidal wave. Okuninushi was no dummy—these gods were powerful and he knew it. So, after consulting with his sons (and after watching the gods beat one of them up), he agreed to cede power peacefully. In return, he was made a ruler in the world of spirits and was worshipped along with the other gods at one of Japan's greatest temples.

# ANANSI

THE SPIDER

# ANANSI

**TRADITION:** West African

**ALSO KNOWN AS:** Ananse, Kweku Ananse, Aunt Nancy

The world is full of Anansi stories. They seem to have originated among the Ashanti people in Ghana, but have since spread throughout West Africa and the Caribbean and the Americas. As the storytellers have changed, so have the stories, and sometimes even Anansi himself—most radically in the southern United States, where Anansi became the female Aunt Nancy. But Anansi's personality has remained consistent. He is lazy, dishonest, and *very* full of himself. He's also remarkably clever, often finding ways around seemingly impossible challenges. He sneaks and steals and loves a good scheme—he once even faked his own death to score some free food.

But not all of his tricks are bad. In some stories, he just creates the world. In others, he creates people. Sometimes he runs messages between the sky god and the people of Earth. And besides, some of Anansi's targets had it coming.

## ANANSI AND THE SECRET THING

Anansi knew he was clever, and he liked to make sure everyone else knew it, too. He bragged about it to anyone who would listen. One day, he even bragged that he was smarter than the sky god, in this version called Wulbari. When Wulbari heard, he decided to teach Anansi a lesson. He summoned Anansi and told him to go down to Earth and bring him a certain thing. When Anansi asked what he wanted brought back, Wulbari replied that if Anansi was so clever, he should already know.

What could Anansi do? He headed down to Earth. But he didn't start searching for the thing—not right away, that is. First he found some birds and took some of their feathers. Then, safely disguised, he sneaked back up to heaven.

When Wulbari saw Anansi covered in feathers, he thought it was a new sort of bird, and he asked all the other animals what it was called.

\* AHEM \*
"TWEET TWEET"

## Which Sky God?

The vast majority of African religions feature a Supreme Being, an all-powerful creator god who dwells in the sky. His name varies with the language and the culture—he is Mulungu in East Africa, Leza in Central Africa, Nyambe in the southern tropics, and Nyame, Wulbari, Ngewo, Mawu, and Olorun in West Africa, just to name a few. Some are different gods, and some are different names for the same god, and sometimes it can be hard to tell the difference. That's why Anansi stories from different regions give the Supreme Being different names.

None of the animals knew, but one suggested that Anansi might. Wulbari told them he had sent Anansi away for a thing. The animals asked what the thing was, and Wulbari said he hadn't told Anansi, but he was supposed to return with the sun, the moon, and darkness. While the animals laughed at Wulbari's trick, Anansi slipped away and headed back to Earth.

He soon returned with a tightly tied bag. Once everyone was gathered together, he opened it in triumph. First he pulled out darkness, and no one could see anything. Next, he pulled out the moon, and people could see a little. Finally, he pulled out the sun—and everyone who wasn't blinking at the time went blind from the brightness.

## ANANSI AND ALL THE STORIES

One of Anansi's greatest powers is his ability to tell stories. But that power wasn't always his. According to one myth, it originally belonged to the sky god Nyame. Anansi asked to buy it from him, but Nyame said Anansi could never afford something so valuable. But Anansi kept pestering him until finally Nyame named a price: the python, the hornets, the leopard, and the fairy.

Anansi went back home and talked it over with his wife, who told him what to do. First, Anansi found a stick and some vines and walked along a stream until he found the python. He told the python that he and his wife had been arguing about how long the python was, and he asked if he could use the stick to measure it. The python agreed and straightened itself out next to the stick. As soon as it did, Anansi grabbed the vines, tied the python up, and delivered his python-on-a-stick to Nyame.

Next, Anansi filled a gourd full of water, found the hornets, sneaked up, and splashed water all over them. Then he yelled that it was raining and suggested the hornets all get inside the gourd to be safe. When they did, he slammed the lid shut and delivered the hornet-filled gourd to Nyame.

Then Anansi skittered over to where the leopard liked to hang out. He dug a deep hole and covered it with sticks and leaves. Sure enough, the leopard walked past and fell into the trap, and Anansi appeared at the edge to offer his help. He handed down a ladder, but as soon as the leopard reached the top, Anansi slashed him with a knife and dragged him up to Nyame.

...SNEAKY, LYING, LEGGY OLD...

There are lots of versions of the story of Anansi gaining, buying, or stealing the power of storytelling. In one, he sells his own mother!

For the fairy, Anansi carved a little doll and covered it in sticky resin. Then he stuck some mashed yams in its hands and hung it from a tree like a puppet. Soon a fairy appeared and asked the puppet if she could have some of the yams. Anansi made the doll nod. The fairy ate the yams and thanked the doll. But the doll stayed rudely silent. So the fairy slapped it, and her hand stuck to the resin. Anansi took the fairy to Nyame.

SPINDLY, UNTRUSTWORTHY JERK!

When Anansi had brought everything Nyame had demanded, Nyame had no choice but to give Anansi the ability to tell stories. From then on, they were called spider stories.

# APHRODITE

## THE LOVE AND BEAUTY GODDESS

# APHRODITE

**TRADITION:** Greek/Roman
**HOME:** Mount Olympus
**ALSO KNOWN AS:** Venus (Roman)

Aphrodite (pronounced "aff-row-*die*-tee") is good-looking—famously good-looking. But being good-looking isn't always good—especially when you have to deal with endless streams of lovestruck mortals, aggressive gods, and jealous goddesses.

Case in point: The goddess Hera got mad at Aphrodite because Hera's husband, Zeus, tried to seduce her, and Zeus got mad at Aphrodite because she rejected him. Her punishment, a forced marriage with the unsightly smith god, Hephaistos, was as crummy for him as it was for her. She was stuck with the ugliest god as a husband, and he was stuck with the least faithful wife on Mount Olympus. Aphrodite had loads of boyfriends after that, including the gods Hermes, Dionysus, and Ares.

> Another myth says that it wasn't Zeus who made Aphrodite marry Hephaistos, but his wife, Hera. Hephaistos trapped Hera in a custom-made throne and wouldn't let her go until she promised to make Aphrodite his wife.

Sources disagree on Aphrodite's origins. Some say she's the daughter of Zeus and a nymph named Dione. Others claim that she emerged from the sea foam surrounding a piece of a dead god. Either way, she became one of the most popular gods on Mount Olympus. There were temples to Aphrodite all over Greece and Rome.

HAS ANYONE SEEN MY ARMS? I SWEAR THEY WERE HERE A CENTURY AGO...

## PYGMALION'S SULTRY STATUE

Aphrodite was a favorite subject for Greek and Roman artists and the inspiration for one of the world's most famous statues, the Venus de Milo (which still exists today, give or take a couple of arms). There's even a myth about a statue of Aphrodite: The statue was so beautiful that its sculptor, Pygmalion, fell deeply in love with it. He kept the statue with him everywhere—working, shopping, sleeping—and hoped and prayed that it would be his wife. Aphrodite heard his prayers and granted his wish. The statue came to life, and Pygmalion and the statue lived happily ever after.

## ADONIS, WHAT A BABE!

Once, a princess named Myrrha claimed she had better hair than Aphrodite. Unfortunately for her, Aphrodite heard about it. She punished Myrrha with a horrible curse: She would fall in love with her own dad.

Under the influence of the curse, Myrrha disguised herself and seduced her father. When he finally realized who she was, Myrrha's dad was horrified. He chased her out of the house and into a field, sword raised, ready to kill her. Myrrha prayed to the gods to help her disappear, and at the last second they granted her wish and turned her into a tree.

But as it turned out, Myrrha was pregnant. Soon the tree gave birth to Adonis, the most beautiful baby who ever lived. Aphrodite fell in love with Adonis at once. She scooped him up, stuck him in a chest, and left it with the queen of the under-world, Persephone, for safekeeping.

When Aphrodite left, Persephone peeked inside the chest and saw Adonis. She fell in love just like Aphrodite had. The two goddesses pleaded and argued and fought with each other over who got to keep Adonis, but neither would budge, until Zeus mandated a solution. For a third of the year, Adonis would live with Aphrodite. For another third, he would stay with Persephone. And for the final third, he could do whatever he wanted.

### Horses and Heels

Two common turns of phrase have origins in the story of the Troy: *Trojan horse* and *Achilles' heel*.

A Trojan horse is a harmless-looking gift that conceals danger. (This is also why harmless-looking files containing computer viruses are called trojans.) The phrase comes from the end of the Trojan War, when the Greek armies besieging Troy broke camp and marched away, leaving a huge wooden horse as a parting gift. The Trojans, thinking they won the war, brought the horse into the city to celebrate their victory. But that night, the Greek soldiers who were hiding inside the horse climbed out and opened the city gates, allowing the rest of the Greek army to enter, sack the city, and win the war.

An Achilles' heel is a single, fatal vulnerability. It's named after Achilles, a Greek hero from the Trojan War. When he was a baby, his mother dipped him in magical water that would make him invincible. It washed every part of his body, except the heel she held him by. He grew up to be one of the greatest warriors of his age, undefeated until he was shot in the heel with a poisoned arrow during the Trojan War.

# HOW APHRODITE ACCIDENTALLY DESTROYED TROY

It was the wedding of the century, and all the gods and goddesses were invited—all, that is, except for Eris, the goddess of discord. When Eris tried to come anyway, she was turned away at the door. Furious and humiliated, she tossed a golden apple over the gate and yelled that it was a gift to the fairest goddess (fairest meaning prettiest).

Hera, Athena, and Aphrodite each thought themselves the fairest and got into a fight over the apple. Zeus decided the dispute would be judged by Paris, prince of Troy.

Each goddess tried to sway Paris's decision. Hera offered him power, Athena offered him wisdom, and Aphrodite offered him the most beautiful woman in the world as a wife. To be fair to Paris, this was an impossible situation. The goddesses he didn't choose would be angry, and angry goddesses are no joke. In any case, Paris chose Aphrodite's offer.

On his next trip to Sparta, he met the king's beautiful wife, Helen, and they fell in love. He brought her back to Troy, and the king of Sparta followed them, along with his army, beginning a brutal ten-year war that left Paris dead, Troy destroyed, and wooden horses forever tarnished.

# APOLLO

## THE BRIGHT ONE

# APOLLO

**TRADITION:** Greek/Roman

**HOME:** Mount Olympus

**ALSO KNOWN AS:** Apollon, Phoebus Apollo,
Helios (a sun god with whom Apollo sort of merged)

If knowledge is power, you would be hard-pressed to find a god more powerful than Apollo. Even Athena, the cleverest goddess, can only make educated guesses at the future. Apollo simply knows it. He is the god of prophecy and hidden things, all seeing, all knowing, and always ready to shine his light into the darkness.

If you are virtuous, Apollo is a good friend to have. He can heal your illnesses and protect you from dangers you never saw coming. He might even grant you the power of prophecy. But if you're evil, watch your back—no one can hide from the god of light, and his death-bringing arrows rarely miss.

## APOLLO'S BIRTH

Both Apollo and his twin sister, Artemis, were products of one of Zeus's many love affairs. As usual, Zeus's wife, Hera, found out, and she took out her jealous rage on the other woman, a goddess named Leto. She sent a huge snake named Python to torture Leto to death. With Zeus's help, Leto transformed into a bird and escaped, but Leto's troubles weren't over. Bird or not, she was pregnant.

Leto flew all across Greece, searching for somewhere to land and give birth. But wherever she went, Hera got there first. Eventually, Leto found the tiny, harsh island of Delos. The residents of Delos were reluctant to accept her—they didn't want to attract Hera's rage—but when they realized how much wealth and prestige their island would get as the birthplace of a god, they allowed her to land. Leto, now human again, went into labor for nine days. First she gave birth to the goddess of the hunt, Artemis, and then, with Artemis's help, to Apollo.

## The Oracle at Delphi

Delphi was one of the most important places in ancient Greece. It was home to the oracle, a priestess who had the power to deliver prophecies from Apollo himself. People would travel for weeks and bring magnificent gifts for a chance to ask her about their future.

Once they arrived, they made their offerings, asked their questions, and then waited as the oracle settled into a trance. She spoke the prophecy whenever it came, with attending priests scribbling notes on what she said and what it might mean. The advice was always accurate, but it wasn't always clear. Emperor Croesus of Lydia once asked the oracle whether he should go to war with Persia and learned that if he did, he would destroy a great empire. The prediction, as always, was correct—but the empire he destroyed was his own.

## APOLLO'S YEAR ABROAD

Apollo's first act as a god was to track down Python and kill it. But Python was a child of the earth goddess Gaia, and you can't kill a goddess's kid without punishment. So Apollo was sentenced to spend a year as a shepherd for King Admetus of Pherae in Thessaly.

King Admetus was a good man, and by the end of his service, Apollo was so impressed by the king's generosity that he offered him any gift he wanted. When Admetus said he didn't need any payment, Apollo promised instead to help him in the future, then vanished.

Some time later, Admetus fell in love with Alcestis, a princess from a neighboring kingdom. But Alcestis's father said he would only allow their marriage if Admetus rode a chariot pulled by a lion and a boar. So Admetus called in his favor, and Apollo showed up to wrestle the beasts into a chariot and help Admetus drive it. Alcestis's father wasn't happy, but a deal was a deal, and the two were married. As a wedding present, Apollo gave Admetus another fine gift: immortality—sort of. When it came time for Admetus to die, he could postpone his death if someone else agreed to die in his place.

After many happy years of marriage, Admetus fell ill, and no one, not even his elderly parents, would agree to die in his place.

As he approached the end, Admetus lost consciousness . . . and then woke up, totally cured. He ran through his palace to tell his beloved Alcestis, only to find that it was she who had died so he could live. Admetus stayed by Alcestis's body for days, heartbroken and refusing to sleep or eat.

Alcestis's spirit, meanwhile, caught the notice of Queen Persephone of the underworld—after all, it's not every day that a soul dies willingly for another. When she learned of the sacrifice Alcestis had made, Persephone was so moved that she sent Alcestis back. Color returned to her previously dead body, and she opened her eyes in the world of the living. Alcestis and Admetus lived happily ever after.

## THE BATTLE OF THE BARDS

As a god of music, Apollo is the best lute player this side of Mount Olympus. Once, a satyr named Marsyas challenged him to a music contest. (A satyr is a creature in Greek and Roman mythology that's half goat, half man, and as playful as he is violent.) Apollo accepted and the Muses, goddesses of the arts, agreed to judge. Marsyas went first, and his flute was sweet and pure. Then Apollo came out with his lute and blew everyone away with his divine music. The muses declared Apollo the winner, and Apollo tore his opponent, Marsyas, to pieces.

# ARTEMIS

## THE VIRGIN HUNTRESS

# ARTEMIS

**TRADITION:** Greek/Roman
**HOME:** Deep in the wilderness
**ALSO KNOWN AS:** Diana (Roman),
Selene (a moon goddess whom she replaced)

Artemis's mother, Leto, had little trouble delivering her. But when Leto gave birth to Artemis's twin brother, Apollo, it took her nine days. Artemis did her best to help, but her mother's agony made a big impression on the young goddess. She declared that she would never give birth and dedicated her life to helping women—especially girls, virgins, and pregnant women.

Artemis is incredibly nurturing to those she cares for, but don't mistake that for weakness. She's a strong, tough, unforgiving goddess, and few who cross her live to regret it. (That goes for her worshippers too—there are accounts of survivors of shipwrecks making it ashore only to be sacrificed in her honor.)

Artemis is also a goddess of the wilds, the hunt, and the moon, and is a famously good shot with her bow and arrows. For the most part, she avoids male company, and society in general. Instead she wanders the wilderness with her bow, her hunting dogs, and a group of loyal nymphs.

## THE SAD TALE OF BIG BEAR

Artemis protects virgins, but she isn't so kind to women who break their vows of chastity. Just ask Callisto, one of her nymph attendants who had the misfortune of attracting Zeus.

When Artemis discovered that Callisto was pregnant with Zeus's child, she burned with anger, and Zeus's excuses only outraged her more. She transformed Callisto into a bear and drew her bow to hunt her. But Zeus rescued bear-Callisto and her baby from Artemis's arrows, flinging them up into the sky. They are still up there as two constellations: Ursa Major and Ursa Minor, the Big Bear and the Little Bear.

I CAN'T **BEAR** THIS BETRAYAL.

## NO BOYS ALLOWED

Actaeon was a great hunter and for a time a companion of Artemis. One day, he stole a glimpse of Artemis bathing in her sacred spring. Unfortunately for him, Artemis noticed. Her revenge was swift and permanent: She turned Actaeon into a stag and watched as he was torn apart by his own hunting dogs.

## How We Know What We Know About Greek Mythology

Greek myths are some of the best-known legends in the world, thanks almost entirely to the ancient Greeks who wrote them all down. We have tons of sources from throughout their history, and even more from the Romans who worshipped many of the same gods (just with different names). They don't tell the whole story, but here are just a few of the most important sources on Greek mythology.

- **Hesiod's *Theogony*:** Hesiod was a Greek poet from before 700 BCE. His most famous work, *Theogony*, provides a rare overview of ancient myths, including the creation of the world and gods, and one of the most detailed mythological family trees ever written.

- **Homer's *The Iliad* and *The Odyssey*:** These two epic poems, which together tell the story of the Trojan War and its aftermath, are also some of our earliest sources on Greek myth. These works are all about gods and heroes and monsters, and are great (and long) reads.

- **Greek plays:** Greek theater, especially in Athens, included tons of tellings and retellings of myths. Most of these have been lost in the intervening two or three thousand years, but a few survived, and some are even performed today.

- **Greek histories and geographies:** Writers like the Greek historian Herodotus were far more interested in earthly matters than in myths and legends, but many of their works reference myths.

- **Vases and other archeological sources:** Writing isn't the only place to learn about mythology. Ancient Greek vases, statues, paintings, and monuments show images of various mythological scenes, some of which elaborate on the legends we know, and some of which point to ones that we don't.

## The Seven Wonders of the Ancient World

The Temple of Artemis at Ephesus, in Asia Minor (modern-day Turkey), was one of the seven wonders of the ancient world. We don't know much about it, given that it was destroyed almost two thousand years ago, but we do know it was huge and beautiful and covered from floor to ceiling with intricate paintings and sculptures.

The other six wonders of the ancient world (as listed by the Greeks) were the Great Pyramid in Egypt, the Hanging Gardens of Babylon, the statue of Zeus in Olympia, the Mausoleum (or tomb) of Halicarnassus in Persia, the Colossus of Rhodes, and the Great Lighthouse of Alexandria.

# THE MANY DEATHS OF ORION

The son of the sea god Poseidon, Orion was a giant, a skilled hunter, and by all accounts a very, very good-looking guy. After a lifetime of killing, he became one of Artemis's hunting buddies, and that's where stories begin to differ. All of them agree that Orion died, and most agree that Artemis killed him, but there's a lot of variety in the how and why.

In some accounts, Orion attacked one of Artemis's nymphs, or even Artemis herself, and Artemis stopped him—permanently. One version says that Artemis fell in love with Orion and killed him in a jealous rage when she found out he preferred Aurora, goddess of the dawn. Another says Artemis's brother, Apollo, worried that Artemis might be falling for Orion and tricked her into shooting an arrow at something floating way out at sea, which turned out to be Orion's head. And there's another story where Artemis is hardly involved—Orion was killed by a huge scorpion, sent by the earth goddess Gaia.

In any case, Orion wound up honored with a famous constellation.

WHAT A GREAT DAY FOR A SWIM!

# ATEN

**THE SOLAR DISK**

## ATEN

**TRADITION:** Egyptian
**HOME:** The heavens
**ALSO KNOWN AS:** Aton

Ancient Egyptians believed in a lot of gods: war gods, water gods, animal gods, plant gods—and a half-dozen sun gods alone. But for about sixteen years in the fourteenth century BCE, there was only one god—Aten.

Aten started out as a picture of the sun. The sun-disk, or *Aten*, was a common symbol in Egyptian art, usually drawn alongside major sun gods like Ra, Atum, or Amun. Over a couple thousand years, Aten became recognized as a deity in his own right. But even then, he was pretty minor.

Aten got his first big break when a pharaoh, Amenhotep II, made him his family's patron god. Under Amenhotep and his son, Aten worship became more widespread, although he still didn't compare to the most popular gods of the day. But then came Amenhotep IV, or as he liked to call himself, Akhenaten.

## AKHENATEN TALKED TO ATEN IN AKHETATEN

Akhenaten (which probably means "one effective on behalf of Aten") declared that Aten wasn't just a god; he was *the* god, alone and without equal. Akhenaten started construction on a new capital city called Akhetaten and tried to stamp out all traditional religion and mythology. He banned festivals and worship of other gods. He sent troops out to defile temples and erase the other gods' names wherever they could find them. Priests became priests of Aten or unemployed. Or, more accurately, they became priests of Akhenaten. See, the way Akhenaten told it, Aten only gave life to the pharaoh and to the women in the pharaoh's family. Everyone else got life from Akhenaten himself, in return for their total and unconditional loyalty.

WHO'S THIS GOD?

THAT'S NOT A—

I LIKE HIM!

Belief in many gods is called *polytheism*, while belief in only one god is called *monotheism*. Depending how you define it, Akhenaten's religion might have been the first monotheistic religion.

No one is sure why Akhenaten did what he did. Maybe he was a true believer. Maybe it was all just a cynical attempt to gain more power. It might have been both. It might have been neither. Whatever the case, people hated it.

To ancient polytheistic people, all gods were real gods. They might think their god was best, or that your god was worst, or even that your god was actually their god using a different name, but they would never claim your god didn't exist. And if you told them theirs didn't exist, they'd be appalled. They might even take revenge.

Akhenaten told everyone in Egypt that their gods didn't exist. The people went along with it for a while, because Akhenaten also had a bunch of guys with spears who would poke them if they didn't. But after Akhenaten died in 1336 BCE, the people didn't just unreform his reforms—they demonized him, and then they erased him. Within a few hundred years, the whole episode was totally forgotten, until archeologists rediscovered it more than three thousand years later.

# ATHENA

**WISE PATRONESS OF HEROES**

## ATHENA

**TRADITION:** Greek/Roman
**HOME:** Mount Olympus
**ALSO KNOWN AS:** Pallas Athene, Minerva (Roman)

If you ever find yourself facing a perilous journey, impossible task, or deadly monster, you will want to talk to Athena. She is a wise judge, an expert craftswoman, and the best tactician on Mount Olympus.

Athena's wisdom isn't the wisdom of age, experience, folksy lessons, or family remedies. Athena's wisdom is about good judgment, sharp wits, and an impeccable sense of timing. She has a habit of showing up right when she's needed, with solutions that no one even considered. The sea god Poseidon made horses, but Athena invented the bridle. The goddess Demeter might make fields fertile, but Athena provides the plow, the rake, and the plot. Ares, god of war, may be a daring warrior, but Athena is the better strategist. Let the other gods swing their powers around—Athena wins battles before they even start.

## ATHENA VS. ZEUS'S HEAD

Prophecies about unborn babies show up in myths around the world. Sometimes it's good news, and the expectant parents rejoice. But sometimes the prophecy is bad, and people try to stop it. They send the kid (or the pregnant lady) away, or just kill them.

When the king of the gods, Zeus, learned that Metis, goddess of wisdom, might give birth to a god stronger than him, he ate her. Sometime later, he came down with an awful headache. He did his best to ignore it, but the pain was so great that he eventually ordered the smith god Hephaistos to bash his head in, just to make it stop. The moment Hephaistos's ax hit Zeus's skull, Athena burst out. She was fully grown, armed, and armored, and really scared the gods until they realized she was friendly.

## HOW ATHENA INVENTED SPIDERS

Arachne of Colophon was a great weaver, and she knew it. Her designs were so beautiful, her technique so flawless, that people would travel miles to see her work. A rumor started that she was taught by Athena herself—high praise, given that Athena was the goddess of weaving. Most people would have appreciated the compliment. But Arachne rejected it. Not only did Athena not teach her, she said, but she was a better weaver than Athena and dared anyone to prove otherwise.

Imagine her surprise when Athena herself arrived to accept her challenge. They set up their looms and got to work. Athena wove gorgeous scenes of gods looking godly, along with a few ominous pictures of what happened to mortals who crossed them. Arachne, meanwhile, wove images of gods doing things with mortals that embarrassed everyone involved.

Arachne's weaving was as flawless as ever, but the images were insulting, so Athena beat her up and left. A while later, Arachne tried to hang herself, but Athena was still too mad to let her die. She turned Arachne into the first spider, so she would be stuck hanging and weaving forever.

## HOW ATHENA WON ATHENS

Athena is the patron goddess of Athens—that's why it's called Athens. But that wasn't always the case. Long ago, when Athens was first settled, it didn't have a patron god. The gods of Olympus knew it would be a great city, and they had a big argument over who would get it. Eventually, they narrowed it down to two options: Poseidon, because the city was near the ocean, and Athena, because she was a goddess of crafts, skills, and civilization. Neither side was willing to give, so Zeus announced a contest: Whoever could create the best new invention for humanity would get the city.

Poseidon hit the ground once with his trident and out sprang a huge animal: the world's first horse. It was strong and fast enough to outrun any man, yet docile enough to ride. The gods were impressed. What could be more useful than this?

Then Athena smiled and showed the gods her work: an olive tree. She explained that it was a hardy tree, able to grow almost anywhere. Its fruit would feed people, and its oil would be used in sacrifices to the gods. More than that, while a horse represents war, an olive tree represents peace—and surely peace is more useful to humanity than war.

The judges of the contest agreed, and the city was named Athens in Athena's honor. Her temple, the Parthenon, was built on its highest hill.

### Athena the Hero-Helper

Athena has a soft spot for heroes and adventurers, especially those who find clever ways to achieve their goals. When Athena speaks, wise heroes listen, because if it weren't for Athena, Greek mythology would have a lot fewer heroes and a lot more hero sandwiches. Here are some famous heroes that Athena has helped.

| Hero: | What Athena did: |
| --- | --- |
| Achilles | Caught and killed Hector of Troy, who killed Achilles' friend |
| Jason and his Argonauts | Directed construction on the boat they used in their quest for the Golden Fleece |
| Theseus | Advised him not to get hit by flying trees |
| Perseus | Pointed him to the items he needed to kill Medusa, including the Helm of Hades, which renders its wearer invisible |
| Bellerophontes | Gave him the flying horse Pegasus |
| Heracles | Instructed him in killing and skinning a lion, and scaring some horrible birds |
| Odysseus | Helped countless times on his long journey home from fighting in the Trojan War |

# BAAL

## LORD OF STORMS

# BAAL

**TRADITION**: Semitic

**HOME**: A northern mountain

**ALSO KNOWN AS**: Hadad, Beelzebub (much later)

Baal's name means *Lord*, and he seems to be a combination of a bunch of earlier gods, or "Lords," of various cities in the Middle East. That's the theory, in any case. By the time people chiseled the clay tablets that gave us most of our knowledge of Baal, around 1500 BCE, he was already a fully formed deity in his own right. He wasn't the head of his pantheon—that's El, the creator. But because Baal brought the rain that farmers depended on, he was the most important.

## BAAL FIGHTS THE OCEAN

Some gods are born with their powers, but not Baal. He won his from Yamm, the Prince of the Sea, a primordial god of floods and chaos.

A long, long time ago, Yamm decided to become king of the gods. El, the creator, said he would allow it, but only if Yamm could defeat Baal. So Yamm sent messengers to Baal and demanded his surrender. Baal responded by attacking the messengers and then Yamm himself, using magical weapons forged by divine smiths.

After a climactic battle, Baal defeated Yamm and stripped him of his power over water. And that was a good thing, at least as far as humans were concerned. Instead of flooding everything, like Yamm did, Baal used this power to help people grow crops.

### The Lord of the Flies

Baal has stayed relevant in some modern religions, although probably not in the way he would have hoped. In one section of the Hebrew Bible, the prophet Elijah yells at a king for consulting priests of Baal Zebub, "Lord of the Flies." (This was possibly a distortion of "Lord of the House," or even a way of calling Baal a poop god.) Things only got worse for Baal after that. By the time the New Testament of the Bible was written, Baal Zebub had become Beelzebub, another name for Satan.

## BAAL FIGHTS DEATH

Defeating Yamm gave Baal a huge amount of power, so he asked El for a home befitting his new importance. El ordered Kothar, the craftsman of the gods, to build Baal a beautiful palace. Once it was done, Baal invited all the gods to a celebratory feast, with the exception of Mot, the god of death. Mot repaid the insult by sneaking into Baal's new palace and formally inviting him to dine in the underworld. Baal didn't want to go, but the gods' rules of etiquette meant he had no choice but to graciously accept the invitation.

As Mot had planned, eating the food of the underworld bound Baal there. Without the storm god's power, rain stopped falling, plants stopped growing, and famine struck the earth.

Luckily, Baal's sister Anath came to the rescue. She charged into the underworld, cut Mot in half, skinned him, burned him, ground him up, and planted the bits in the ground like seeds. Then she returned Baal to the world of the living.

But it takes more than death to kill the god of the underworld. Soon enough Mot returned to life. He and Baal met in combat and fought each other to a stalemate. It only ended when the other gods intervened and separated them, sending Mot back to the underworld and Baal back to his palace.

This myth makes sense if you think of it as a farming metaphor: Every year, there's a wet season (represented by Baal) and a dry season (represented by Mot). In the dry season, when Mot has imprisoned Baal, farmers do to their grain what Anath did to Mot: cut it, thresh it, grind and cook some, and plant the rest for the following year. Then Baal returns to his palace, and the wet season returns.

SO...WILL YOU BE STAYING LONG?

# BALDR

## THE TRAGIC SON

# BALDR

**TRADITION:** Norse
**HOME:** Asgard
**ALSO KNOWN AS:** Balder, Baldur

Baldr is a bit of an enigma, mythologically speaking. We only have two sources on him, and they each say different things. In one myth, he's a beloved god, killed by a cruel trick. In another, he's a human warrior, cut down in battle against a worthy foe.

## A GOD NAMED BALDR

The best-known version of the Baldr story comes from Iceland. Baldr was the bright, kind, charismatic son of the high god Odin and his wife, Frigg, and everyone loved him. When he was a baby, Frigg brought him around to everyone and everything, and each in turn promised not to hurt him—each, that is, except the mistletoe, which was so tiny and harmless that no one thought to ask.

Baldr grew up happy, beautiful, and invincible. The gods even made a game out of throwing stuff at him and watching it miss or bounce off harmlessly. The only one who didn't play was Baldr's brother, Hodr, and that was just because he was blind.

According to an old Norse folk belief, things get damp after a frost thaws because everyone and everything is weeping for Baldr.

One day, while they played, the god Loki showed up with a package and sidled over to Hodr. He could see that Hodr wanted to play, Loki said, and he wanted to help. He even brought a special arrow, just for Hodr to use. Hodr excitedly accepted. He nocked the arrow, pulled the string, and, with Loki's hand guiding his aim, released his shot. Imagine the rest of the gods' surprise and dismay as they saw Baldr fall, a mistletoe arrow buried deep in his chest.

Everyone was grief-stricken, especially Frigg. She went all the way to Hel (the Norse underworld) to ask Hel (the goddess of the Norse underworld) for her son back. Usually, dead folks didn't get to leave the underworld, but Hel made a deal with Frigg. If everyone and everything cried for Baldr, she would return him to the world of the living.

So once again, Frigg went around to everyone and everything, this time to ask them to cry for Baldr. Everyone and everything in the world cried, except for one old, cantankerous lady. It's not exactly spelled out in the myth, but there's a theory that the old lady might have been Loki in disguise. But disguise or no, a deal was a deal, and Baldr stayed dead.

CAREFUL, NOW— WOULDN'T WANT TO MISS!

## A HERO NAMED BALDR

In the other version of the story, from Denmark, Baldr and Hodr weren't gods or brothers, but human warriors who fought over a girl named Nanna. Baldr got help from a group of Valkyries, who prepared special food that made him invincible. But Hodr also met the Valkyries, and they granted him a belt that would ensure victory and instructions on where to find a powerful sword.

Hodr went on a terrible journey through a freezing, dark land and fought a beast named Mimingus in order to retrieve the sword. Then he returned, fought Baldr, married Nanna, fought Baldr a few more times, and eventually wounded him badly enough that he died.

So Hodr won . . . except not really. Baldr's patron god, Odin, avenged his death by wooing a princess and producing a son, Boe, who grew up and killed Hodr back.

Valkyries are female warrior spirits in the service of Odin. You're most likely to encounter them ferrying the spirits of heroes killed in battle to Odin's great hall, Valhalla. If you're lucky enough to be one of those heroes, you'll also find them serving food and drinks in between dead-hero training sessions, or fighting alongside you at Ragnarok, the battle that will end the world.

LEMME GO! I ALMOST HAD HIM!

# BRAHMA

## THE CREATOR

# BRAHMA

**TRADITION:** Hindu
**HOME:** Brahmaloka

rahma, the serene creator of the universe, has seen better days. Over the past few thousand years, his partners in the Trimurti (the chief triad of Hindu deities), Vishnu and Shiva, have each become the highest god in a major branch of Hinduism. Brahma, meanwhile, has been in decline. Ancient myths that describe Brahma's universe-creating power have gradually fallen away, replaced by newer ones where he is inferior to Vishnu, Shiva, or the great goddess Devi. Nowadays, depending who you ask, he isn't even the actual creator—in fact, one version claims he was born from Vishnu's belly button.

## BRAHMA'S UNIVERSAL DREAM

Unlike in many other creation myths, the Hindu universe didn't begin with a void. It began with a formless, eternal, universal consciousness called Brahman. At some point, Brahman realized it wanted to create something. It willed into existence some primordial waters, and then a seed. The seed grew into a bright, shining, golden egg, and inside the egg was Brahma. For a year, nothing happened. But then Brahma's meditation split the egg smoothly around the middle. The top half became the sky and the bottom half the earth, and Brahma remained in the middle, meditating. Every single object in the material world, and every thought and concept we use to understand that world, emerged from Brahma's meditation.

OOoMMM....

OOoMMM....

MMMM....

## THE STORY OF BRAHMA'S HEADS

You might have noticed that Brahma has four heads. But according to one story, he started with just one.

When Brahma created his wife, Saraswati, he thought she was the most beautiful person he had ever seen. He wanted to look at her all the time, but she didn't enjoy being stared at constantly.

She tried to dodge out of sight, first to the left, then to the right, and then behind him. But each time she left his vision, Brahma grew a new head to keep staring. In exasperation, she leaped into the sky, but Brahma sprouted a fifth head to look up. Later, the god Shiva shot the fifth head off, leaving Brahma with four.

## Cosmic Timekeeping

In Hinduism, time is infinite. It has no beginning or end, just cycles of creation and destruction that repeat forever. The length of these cycles is based on Brahma's life span, which is a hundred years. But don't worry—they are really, really long years.

Here's how it works:

1 year of Brahma's life is 360 kalpas, or Brahma days

1 kalpa is 1,000 mahayugas, or great ages

1 mahayuga is split into 4 yugas (ages), of differing lengths:

> The Satya yuga, a golden age, lasting 1,728,000 human years
>
> The Treta yuga, a mostly moral age, lasting 1,296,000 human years
>
> The Dvapara yuga, a half-moral age, lasting 864,000 human years
>
> The Kali yuga, a mostly awful age, lasting 432,000 human years (this is the one we are in now)

After that, the world is destroyed and a new age begins.

So how long does the universe last? Depends what you mean by *universe*. Our universe lasts as long as Brahma's daily meditation, 4.32 billion human years. Once it ends, he gets a 4.32 billion human year rest. Then he starts again, and another universe emerges. This cycle will go on until Brahma himself dies, after a life span of 155,520 billion human years.

But not to worry—the Hindu universe is infinite. After another 155,520 billion human years, a new Brahma will be born, and the cycle will start again.

### Devas and Asuras

The devas are the gods of Hindu mythology, but they don't rule unopposed. They must always stay vigilant against the asuras, violent demons of the underworld.

Usually, asuras are the opposites of the devas. Where devas are humble, asuras are arrogant. Where devas are honest, asuras are cheaters. Where devas are wise and full of compassion, asuras are ignorant and selfish.

But don't make the mistake of thinking all devas are good or all asuras are bad. It's more complicated than that. Some ancient texts even call certain gods both devas and asuras, and there have been times when the two have worked together toward common goals. It might be best to think of them like this: Asuras are agents of chaos and trickery, and devas are pillars of order.

## A TALE OF THREE CITIES

In more recent stories, Brahma has lost so much esteem that he is forced to grant wishes. Such is the case in this story.

Three asura brothers put themselves through such intense spiritual training that they earned a wish from Brahma. They wished first for invulnerability, but Brahma said he couldn't grant them that—nothing is invulnerable to everything. So instead they wished to rule three cities for a thousand years and then bring them together into one super-city that could only be destroyed by the best of the gods. Brahma had no choice but to grant their wish.

Three cities were established: a city of gold in the heavens, a city of silver in the air, and a city of iron on Earth. Over the centuries, the cities filled with asuras, drawn by the wealth and power within. But after their thousand years were up, the god Shiva got sick of their moral failings. He burned their cities and their residents to ash and flung whatever was left into the ocean.

WISHES GRANTED

# COYOTE

## TRICKSTER OF THE SOUTHWEST

## COYOTE

**TRADITION:** Southwestern North America

oyote spans a wide range of cultures. While most of his myths come from the American Southwest, there are records of Coyote from all across the continent. He is the classic trickster god: quick-witted, greedy, and lazy. Sometimes he creates things, but more often he wrecks them, and he's as likely to get himself into trouble as out of it.

## COYOTE TRICKS PEOPLE

Coyote has a starring role in the creation story of the Maidu people of California. In their telling, Coyote didn't make the world—two other gods, named Turtle and Earth Initiate, did. They made the sun and the stars, and then sculpted people and animals out of clay. While they worked, Coyote and his pet, Rattlesnake, would sit to the side and watch.

One day, Coyote decided to try making some beings, too. But he couldn't finish a single sculpture without breaking down laughing, so none of his creations worked. Earth Initiate suggested that if only Coyote stopped laughing, he might make something good. But Coyote insisted that he hadn't laughed at all, telling the world's first lie in the process.

The people Earth Initiate created led easy, lazy lives. They mostly just ate and slept until they grew old. Then they washed in a magical lake and came out with their youth restored, ready to eat and sleep again.

Naturally, Coyote ruined it. He visited them and offered to show them things they had never seen: competition, sickness, and death. The people had no idea what he was talking about, but they invited him to show them.

Coyote started by teaching them competition. He lined them all up for a footrace and told them the rules, but didn't mention the venomous rattlesnake hiding along the track. Midway through the race, as the runners sprinted past, Rattlesnake sprang out and bit the lead runner, who crumpled to the ground and died. The rest of the people assumed he was just embarrassed that he fell and tried to cheer him up. Coyote laughed and laughed, until he got close enough to see who Rattlesnake killed. It was Coyote's own son. Coyote tried dunking him in the youth-restoring lake, but it didn't revive him or anyone else ever again.

## COYOTE TRICKS A GIANT

Navajo folklore says that long ago, giants walked the earth—and stomped, and yelled, and ate all the children they could catch. One day Coyote ran into one of these giants and decided to punish him.

Coyote convinced the giant to build a sweat lodge. Once it was ready and full of steam, Coyote said he would perform a miracle: He would break his own leg and then magically unbreak it.

He sneaked a dead deer's leg into the lodge and hit it with a rock until it broke. It was far too steamy to see, but the giant could feel that the leg was broken. Then Coyote spat on the leg, chanted, and quietly shoved the deer leg out of the way. When the giant reached over and felt again, he found Coyote's leg, safe and sound and unbroken. He was impressed!

So when Coyote offered to repeat the miracle on the giant, the giant happily agreed. Coyote used his rock to break the giant's leg, and said all the giant had to do was spit on it. The giant spat and spat, but his leg didn't heal. Coyote encouraged him to just keep spitting and quietly slipped out of the lodge.

KEEP ON SPITTING!

## COYOTE TRICKS HIMSELF

The Sioux have a story in which Coyote gets what's coming to him, and then some.

As Coyote and his friend walked one day, they ran into a wise and powerful rock named Iya. Coyote had heard that Iya could tell a good story. To show his respect, Coyote left a blanket as a gift. But later that day it got cold and rainy, and Coyote went and took his blanket back—even though both his friend and the rock told him not to.

NO TAKEBACKS, COYOTE.

Coyote and his friend found a cave to hide in while they waited out the storm. Suddenly, through the sound of the rain, they heard a faint rumbling. As they listened, it grew louder and louder, and they looked up to see Iya, the rock, crashing through trees and brambles and heading straight toward them. They dropped their food and ran, the rock close on their heels. They found water and swam across, but the rock kept coming. They fled into a deep forest, but the rock just knocked down the trees. Coyote's friend told Coyote it was all his fault, turned into a spider, and hid in a hole. Before Coyote could respond, the rock caught up, flattened him, took the blanket, and left.

A while later, a man wandered by and mistook Coyote for a rug. He took it home to put in front of his fire. But the next day his wife caught the "rug" running away—Coyote's immortal, after all.

NO TAKEBACKS, COYOTE!

# CÚ CHULAINN

## THE GREATEST HERO OF IRELAND

# CÚ CHULAINN

**TRADITION:** Celtic
**HOME:** Ulster, Ireland
**ALSO KNOWN AS:** Cuhullin, Sétanta

Celtic heroes all have a few things in common. They are brave, beautiful, violent men, skilled in combat and magic. They barge into places, take what they like, and break what they like. And while they do protect their people, they're still big scary bullies about it.

There was Fergus mac Róich, a giant with a sword as long as a rainbow, who could eat a whole village's worth of animals in a single sitting. And Conall Cernach, whose name meant "strong as a wolf" and who decorated his belts with the heads of his enemies. But of all the Celtic heroes, the greatest was Cú Chulainn (pronouced "coo *hull*-an").

He was so strong that he scattered entire armies, so brave that he once invaded the underworld itself, and so good-looking that his own countrymen tricked him into leaving the kingdom just to keep him away from their wives. He wielded the *gáe bulg*, a barbed spear that inflicted fatal wounds. And in the heat of battle he could transform himself into a fire-breathing monster, his muscles inflating like balloons, one eye sinking into his head while the other bulged outward.

There are far more stories about Cú Chulainn than could fit in this book, but here are a few of the most interesting.

## CÚ CHULAINN'S TRIPLE BIRTH

Celtic myths are really into threes—folks with three heads, folks with three forms, or folks who did things thrice. Cú Chulainn, for instance, had three birthdays.

Birth #1: Once, a flock of hungry birds ruined the fields around Emain Macha (an ancient town in Northern Ireland), and the warriors of Ulster assembled to fight them off. Nine chariots went out, including that of King Conchobar and his sister Dechtire.

The sun set as they chased the birds past Brug na Bóinne, the most famous fairy mound in Ireland and home to a good-natured god called the Dagda. The charioteers came upon a tiny cottage and asked the couple who lived there if they could stay the night. They were welcomed and, upon entering, were amazed to find that this little cottage was large enough to house and feed the whole group.

That night, the couple of the cottage had a baby. But when the warriors woke up in the morning, the couple and the cottage had vanished. All that was left was the baby, freezing in the morning air. Dechtire tried to save it, but the baby died.

Birth #2: The following night, the god Lug came to Dechtire in a dream. Dechtire woke up pregnant, but that baby died, too.

Birth #3: Dechtire got pregnant again, and this time the baby survived.

The baby's name wasn't Cú Chulainn—that was a title he earned later. As a child, he was called Sétanta.

> At the same time as Cú Chulainn's first birth, two foals were born, the Gray of Macha and the Black of Saingliu. These later became his chariot horses and stayed with him throughout his life.

## SÉTANTA'S CHILDHOOD

Most kids in ancient Celtic cultures were born to one family and parented by another family, which allowed them to learn new skills and trades and helped bond their families and communities together. Sétanta was parented by his whole village, as well as several of the greatest heroes of his age and at least one god.

Sétanta was a brash kid. As a boy, he went to join the king's youth brigade, a sort of ancient Irish boot camp. On his first day, he defeated all 150 of the other boys and placed them all under his protection.

A couple of years later, he overheard a prophecy that whoever took up arms on that day would have a short but glorious life. Sétanta wanted that life. He took up and broke fifteen sets of weapons before demanding, and being granted, the weapons of King Conchobar himself.

## WHY CÚ CHULAINN CAN'T EAT A DOG

So where did Cú Chulainn get his name? In his village, there was a smith named Culann whose workshop was guarded by a monstrous hound. It was a huge beast that took nine men to leash, and it did such a good job guarding that if anyone dared go outside at night it would "guard" them to death. That is, until the night Sétanta got locked out of his house. When the hound came for him, Sétanta went into a rage and threw a ball so far down the dog's throat that it died instantly.

In the morning, the smith was furious, but Sétanta was such an honorable young man that he offered to guard the workshop in the dog's stead. And that's how he got the name Cú Chulainn: "The Hound of Culann." It's also how he got his most famous *geis*, forbidding him to eat dog flesh—ever. If he did, he would die.

CATCH!

### Geis vs. Geese

In Irish mythology a *geis* is a magical bond or obligation. A person's power depended on not breaking any geis. The more powerful you were, the more *geasa* (plural of geis) you had. A major chief might have dozens, from standard chiefly duties like "don't let armies enter your domain unopposed" to more specific ones like "don't cross that river" or "don't eat geese." *Geese* is the plural of *goose*, a migrating bird that produces several pounds of poop daily.

## CÚ CHULAINN EATS A DOG

Medb, queen of Connacht, hated Cú Chulainn, because he kept kicking her armies' butts. So she brought together the children of all the heroes and leaders he had killed and hatched a plan to get rid of him once and for all, by forcing him to break his geasa.

A short while later, on his way to a battle, Cú Chulainn was stopped by three girls roasting a dog. They offered him some. It was geis for Cú Chulainn to eat dog, but it was also geis for him to refuse hospitality. Facing a no-win situation, he chose the tastier option. As he bit into the roast dog, his huge muscles weakened and withered.

Next he encountered a group led by a sorcerer who threatened to curse him if he didn't hand over his spear. He agreed and handed it over as hard as he could, driving it through the sorcerer and several of his warriors and killing them all. After that, he met another sorcerer who demanded his other spear. Once again, Cú Chulainn complied.

Cú Chulainn arrived at the battle weakened and spearless, and though he killed many warriors, he ultimately lost. Mortally wounded, he staggered up a hill and tied himself to a tree so he could die standing, facing his enemies. Even as his life faded, his foes dared not approach—not until the Morrígan, goddess of war, landed on his shoulder in the form of a crow, signaling the death of the Hound of Chulainn.

# THE DAGDA

## THE GOOD GOD

# THE DAGDA

**TRADITION:** Celtic

**HOME:** The Otherworld

**ALSO KNOWN AS:** Sucellos (a Gaulish god who is very similar)

The Dagda is the chieftain of the Tuatha Dé Danann, an ancient race of gods who drove an ancienter race of gods out of Ireland and were later driven out themselves by human beings. His name means *The Good God*, but that might not mean what you think it means.

It's not that the Dagda is morally good (though he is a decent guy by ancient Celtic standards). It's that he's really good at being a god: defending his people and providing for them. He's good at defending thanks to his size, his strength, and his weapon: a club so big that he drags it on wheels. One end brings death to anyone it hits, and the other brings dead people back to life. He's a great provider, both because he's friendly and generous and because his enormous cauldron magically produces enough food that no one leaves a meal unsatisfied.

**CHURL:** One of the lowest, poorest peasants in Irish society. In medieval times, rich folks could afford clothes so long they dragged on the ground. A churl was lucky to cover his bottom. *Churl* is the root of the modern word *churlish*, which means rude and surly.

## WHY THE DAGDA IS A GLUTTON

If you think the Dagda looks funny, you aren't alone—the Celts did, too. He is big and brutish, and his tunic is shorter than the average churl's. Warriors of the time wielded spears, slings, and bows, but the Dagda carries a Stone Age club.

How did the leader of the gods get so big? Ancient cultures demanded that their leaders prove their worth in all sorts of ways, and that included winning the Celtic version of a hot-dog-eating contest. The Dagda might be a total glutton, but by eating, he proves his vitality and ability to provide.

SQUEAK SQUEAK

## How We Know What We Know About Celtic Mythology

Some popular works on Celtic mythology can make it seem like we know tons about it, with long and detailed descriptions of gods, goddesses, creatures, and places. But the truth is, despite the best efforts of scholars, we know very little. The pre-Christian inhabitants of western Europe didn't have a written language, and their priests, the druids, were against committing sacred things to text. As a result, even our best sources are secondhand, written by the Celts' foreign observers or local descendants. Here are the major sources we still have:

- **Roman sources:** Most prominently, "De Bello Gallico," Julius Caesar's account of his conquest of Gaul (modern-day France) in the fifties BCE. Thanks to the Romans' habit of assuming foreign gods were just versions of their own gods, these are biased sources. But they are also the most thorough sources we have for the ancient Celts of mainland Europe.

- **Christian monks:** Starting around 600 CE, Christian monks in Ireland began writing books of ancient stories, including many local sagas. But these, too, can be a bit dodgy. We can't say for sure how much these stories were influenced by the Romans, the later Germanic invaders, or the agendas of the monks themselves.

- **Archeological sources:** By studying the few artifacts the ancient Celts left behind, scholars have begun to put together a clearer picture of their religions and mythology.

## THE TIME THE DAGDA ATE ALL THE PORRIDGE

The Tuatha Dé Danann weren't the first supernatural beings in Ireland. That honor belongs to the Fomorians, who are variously depicted as monsters, giants, and jerks. Their wars with the Tuatha Dé Danann form a big part of Irish mythology.

During these battles (specifically, just before the Second Battle of Magh Tuireadh), the Dagda was sent to gather information on the Fomorians. When he arrived at their camp, they called a temporary truce and invited him in. But just because they weren't fighting didn't mean they planned to be nice.

After they were driven from Ireland by the first humans, the Tuatha Dé Danann were assigned homes by the Dagda in the various mounds and hills across Ireland. Some of these mounds still exist and are supposedly hot spots for fairy activity to this day.

The key to their plan was the Dagda's well-known love of porridge. They boiled eighty measures of milk, meal, and fat, and added eight goats, eight sheep, and eight pigs. When the porridge was hot and ready, they dumped it all in a hole in the ground, brought the Dagda over, and told him to eat it all or be killed.

Their mistake was in underestimating the Dagda's appetite. He pulled out a ladle so big it could fit two people inside and ate all the porridge. At this point the story gets pretty gross in describing his giant, distended belly. It gets even weirder when, belly and all, he manages to charm one of the Fomorians' daughters so much that she promises to turn her magic against her own people.

# DRAGONS

## AND OTHER MYTHICAL REPTILES

Countless mythological creatures have been called dragons, but in most cases *dragon* is a bit of a misnomer. *Dragon* is an English word that English speakers have given to a wide variety of mythical reptiles and snakes over the centuries. A Chinese dragon has as much to do with a European dragon as Chinese checkers has to do with European checkers—there are some similarities, sure, but they are hardly the same thing. Keep that in mind as you read about these dragons and "dragons" from around the world.

> SSSSO EXCITED TO SSSSEE YOU AGAIN, SSSSETH...

## APEP (OR APOPHIS)

The ancient Egyptians believed that the universe was under constant assault by a huge snake creature called Apep, or Apophis in Greek. When the sun god's boat descended from the sky at sunset and began its nightly journey through the underworld, Apep would strike, fangs bared, trying to take down the sun god and plunge the world back into primordial chaos.

Fortunately, the sun god Ra was never alone on the boat—he was aided by other gods who stood with weapons at the ready to stab Apep until he was good and dead. But Apep never stayed dead for long. Each night, like clockwork, he attacked all over again.

## CHINESE DRAGONS

In Chinese mythology, dragons are long, twisty, snakelike beasts with whiskers and legs. They fly through the sky with unearthly grace, often bringing with them rain and storms.

Ancient Chinese texts describe a wide variety of dragon species. The most famous was the long (*long* is a Chinese word for dragon). It had deer antlers, carp scales, cow ears, eagle claws, and bright, demonic eyes. Because of their association with power, wisdom, and good fortune, dragons were frequently adopted as symbols of emperors.

## FAFNIR

The Norse dragon Fafnir wasn't always a beast. In his youth, he was a dwarf prince. Iceland's *Völsunga Saga* tells how Fafnir's father, Hreidmar, forced the god Loki to pay him a fortune in gold. Loki obliged, but the gold he provided was cursed. It would eventually lead to the death of anyone who held on to it. Soon, Hreidmar died, killed by Fafnir in pursuit of the same gold.

MINE... MINE... ALL MINE...

Over time, Fafnir became meaner and greedier, and jealously guarded his stolen treasure. His greed transformed him into a horrible, scaly, poison-breathing dragon. Fafnir died, finally, on the sword of a hero named Sigurd, who was hired by Fafnir's own brother to steal the gold again.

## THE HYDRA

Long ago, the swamps of Lernaea, in Greece, were ravaged by a huge, nine-headed water snake called the Hydra. The hero Heracles was sent to kill the monster. He lured her out of her lair and then jumped onto her, slicing her heads off one by one, but for each head he sliced off, two more grew back. Heracles might have lost the battle and his life if his buddy Iolaus hadn't jumped in. Torch in hand, Iolaus burned the Hydra's wounds before more heads emerged. Eventually only one head was left. This one couldn't be killed, so they knocked the Hydra out, buried her, and put a boulder on top. No one ever saw the Hydra again.

## JÖRMUNGANDR

Jörmungandr is the monstrous snake child of Loki that grew so large it could circle the entire world. Once, while fishing, Thor nearly caught Jörmungandr, but his companion cut the fishing line before he could kill the beast. Thor was angry, but it's a good thing he was stopped. If Thor and Jörmungandr ever actually come to blows, Ragnarok, the battle that ends the world, will begin. During Ragnarok, Thor will smash Jörmungandr to pieces with his hammer but die soon after from Jörmungandr's deadly poison.

## THE RAINBOW SNAKE

Appearing in paintings and inscriptions going back more than six thousand years, the Australian Rainbow Snake is one of the world's oldest mythological creatures. It's a massive water snake, with a long body and a kangaroo-like head. It lives in deep bodies of water and can bring life-giving rain or life-ending disasters.

## SAINT GEORGE'S DRAGON

One of the most iconic dragons in western Europe was the beast killed by Saint George. It was a big, scaly lizard that lived by a lake, killing people and poisoning their lands. It forced the locals to feed it sheep, and when they ran out of sheep, it demanded their children.

One day Saint George came along, armor gleaming in the light, and found a local princess dressed in a wedding gown by the lake. She tried to send him away, but he refused to leave. When the dragon came out of its lair to eat her, Saint George charged it on horseback and stabbed it with his lance, wounding it terribly. Then he took the bride's belt and wrapped it around the beast's neck, walked it into town, and said he would kill it, but only if everyone became Christian.

## ZMEY GORYNYCH

Slavic folklore tells of a flying, fire-breathing monster with three heads called Zmey Gorynych, who battled a legendary Russian knight named Dobrynya Nikitich. When he first encountered the dragon, Dobrynya agreed to spare its life. After Dobrynya rode away, however, the dragon kidnapped a noble maiden named Zabava, so Dobrynya returned to face the dragon again.

It took Dobrynya three days and three hours (and a little advice from the Christian God) to kill Zmey Gorynych. When the creature was dead, Dobrynya found himself stuck in a puddle of the dragon's blood. After three more days, he received some more heavenly advice: to stab his spear into the blood and recite a specific prayer. He did as he was told, and the blood sank into the earth, freeing him to rescue Zabava.

# ENKI

## THE LAW-GIVER

# ENKI

**TRADITION:** Sumerian/Mesopotamian
**HOME:** The Abzu
**ALSO KNOWN AS:** Ea (Akkadian)

It's hard to picture now, but thousands of years ago, cities were new things. And new things meant new problems. It's easy enough to pick a leader when you're a band of twenty people, but what if you're a city of twenty thousand? How do you divide up the land among that many people? The food? The work? How do you protect yourself from raiders? How do you solve disputes? The answer, for the ancient Mesopotamians, was Enki.

Enki is a god of water, laws, and knowledge—especially of crafts and rituals. He's also the creator of the world, humanity, and the rules that govern civilization. One of his most famous myths describes his trip from city to city, region to region, and god to god, telling them what roles they would fill and how they would relate to one another (he initially skips the love and war goddess Inanna, but later gives her the power to "destroy what can't be destroyed").

You can think of Enki as the divine problem solver. When the wind god Enlil tried to kill humanity, Enki found a way to rescue them. When Inanna got trapped in the underworld, Enki found a way to rescue her. When the city of Uruk had a bad king, Enki found a way to depose him.

> ...AND YOU'LL BE GOD OF SANITATION.

## ENKI'S "RELATIONS"

It's not that unusual for the gods to have kids with their cousins, siblings, or even parents. But where familial "relations" are concerned, Enki is in a league all his own. It started with his consort, Ninhursaga, with whom Enki had a daughter named Ninsar. Then Enki went after Ninsar, and she gave birth to Ninkurra. And then Enki went for Ninkurra, who gave birth to Uttu, who by this point was Enki's daughter, granddaughter, and great-granddaughter.

When Enki went after Uttu, Ninhursaga had had enough. She turned what would have been yet another baby goddess into a series of plants—plants that Enki later ate, impregnating himself in the process.

Pregnancy wasn't good for Enki. He didn't have a womb, so the babies grew wherever they could: in his jaw, teeth, mouth, throat, limbs, and ribs. Ninhursaga let him stew for a while before she finally agreed to help. She took the babies into her own body and gave birth to a bunch of goddesses of healing, whom Enki (thankfully) left alone.

> When Enki was pregnant, the baby that grew in his rib was named Ninti, "Lady Rib." Some scholars think she might have been the inspiration for the story in the Bible where the first woman is made from a rib.

## ENKI MAKES PEOPLE

In Mesopotamian mythology, humans weren't the great culmination of creation. They were just solutions to a problem.

It started when the youngest gods went on strike. They were sick of keeping the cosmos going, and they weren't going to do it anymore. Soon the conflict became open war, with the gods picking sides. Abzu, great primordial god of fresh water, tried to destroy the world, but before he could, Enki knocked him out and imprisoned him beneath his city, Eridu. When Abzu's wife, Tiamat, and son, Kingu, tried to finish what Abzu had started, the gods killed them. Tiamat's ribs were used to hold up the sky, and her tail stretched across it as the Milky Way.

The battle was over, but the question remained: If the gods were too lazy to do any work, who would? Enki came up with the solution. He mixed some clay with Kingu's blood and molded it into a person. Once he had shown the other gods how to do it, they made many more humans, secure in the knowledge that the humans would do the work and sustain the gods through worship and sacrifice.

### Abzu Who?

In Sumerian mythology, the Abzu is a huge underground ocean and the source of all fresh water on Earth. It's sometimes described as Enki's home, sometimes as his bodily fluids, and sometimes as a totally separate god of fresh water. Long before the earth existed, Abzu united with the saltwater goddess Tiamat to create a whole bunch of lesser gods.

# ERESHKIGAL

QUEEN OF THE DEAD

# ERESHKIGAL

**TRADITION:** Sumerian/Mesopotamian
**HOME:** Irkalla
**ALSO KNOWN AS:** Allatu (Akkadian)

Irkalla, the ancient Mesopotamian underworld, is a gloomy place. There is no reward or punishment, pleasure or pain. The souls of the dead wander in a boring, colorless imitation of the lives they led on Earth. They just go through the motions, eating dust, drinking mud, needing neither. They are kept in the underworld by seven great gates, and beyond them lies the palace of Ereshkigal.

Ereshkigal is a serious goddess, strong but fair, especially when compared with her more popular sister, the love goddess Inanna. She keeps to herself for the most part and simply does her job: keeping souls confined in Irkalla so they don't go back to haunt the living. But take care: She is very protective of her spiritual subjects. Treat the dead with respect, or you might find she lets one of them out for revenge.

> GODDESS, MY KID JUST DISRESPECTED MY GRAVE.

> OK, GO HAUNT, BUT BE BACK FOR DINNER.

> WE'RE HAVING MUD.

## ERESHKIGAL'S AWFUL SISTER

Ereshkigal's sister Inanna was always a handful. While Ereshkigal was serious and diligent, Inanna was passionate, impetuous, and violent. For the most part, they avoided each other's company, so when Inanna decided to visit Irkalla, Ereshkigal was suspicious.

Inanna came unannounced, banging on Irkalla's outer gates and demanding entry. When Ereshkigal's minister Namtar asked her purpose, she claimed that she had come to mourn her sister's recently deceased husband. Ereshkigal told Namtar to let Inanna in, but to lock the gates behind her, just in case. As was customary, the guards took something from Inanna at each of the seven gates: first her crown, then her earrings, then her necklace, and so on, until she arrived in Ereshkigal's throne room completely naked.

When Ereshkigal stepped down to greet her sister, Inanna pushed past her and sat in Ereshkigal's throne, seizing control of the underworld. But her rule didn't last long. The seven judges of the underworld swept in almost immediately and hit her with their deadly gazes, killing her instantly. They hung her corpse from a hook on the wall, and Ereshkigal returned to her throne.

Back on Earth, Inanna's maidservant, Ninshubur, waited for her return. When Inanna failed to show, Ninshubur followed the instructions Inanna had left. She went to the wind god Enlil and asked him for help, but he angrily refused. If Inanna was so greedy that she tried to steal the underworld, he said, she could stay down there. Ninshubur went next to the moon god Nanna, but received the same response. Finally, she asked the god of wisdom, Enki, and though he complained, he agreed to help.

First, he created two creatures who could enter and leave the underworld at will, and gave them a plant and water that would revive Inanna. Then he told them to sneak into Ereshkigal's palace, where they would find her giving birth (to whom or what, the myth doesn't say). If they kindly mimicked the sounds she made, Ereshkigal would be so thankful for the sympathy that she'd offer them whatever they asked for. All they had to do then was ask for Inanna's corpse.

The creatures did as instructed and brought Inanna back to life. Then, together, they left—almost. The seven judges of the underworld caught up to Inanna and demanded that she find a substitute to die in her place. She considered her servant, Ninshubur, and her hairdresser, Umma, but ultimately settled on her lover, Tammuz.

## ERESHKIGAL'S LOVER

There are two stories explaining how Ereshkigal and the war god Nergal wound up together as king and queen of the underworld.

The older version says that it started with a feast in the heavens. Ereshkigal's duties in the underworld meant she couldn't attend, but she sent her minister Namtar to pick up some food. When Namtar arrived, all the gods stood in respect—all except Nergal. Ereshkigal heard and demanded he be brought to her, so she could teach him a lesson. But the meeting didn't go as planned. Nergal charged through the gates, pulled Ereshkigal off her throne by the hair, and was about to cut her head off when she asked him to marry her instead.

In the second version, Nergal traveled to Ereshkigal's realm because he was fascinated by death. His father, Enki, warned him not to eat or drink anything offered, and especially not to get intimate with Ereshkigal, lest he be trapped there forever. He did all of this anyway, enjoying a week in Ereshkigal's company before making an unlikely escape.

After Nergal left, Ereshkigal missed him terribly and sent her minister Namtar to bring him back. But Enki had cunningly disguised his son as a fool, and Nergal's search was fruitless. Enki needn't have bothered, however, because Nergal missed Ereshkigal, too. It wasn't long before he returned to the underworld, burst through the gates, and pulled Ereshkigal down by her hair, promising to stay with her forever.

# ESHU

## THE MISCHIEVOUS MESSENGER

# ESHU

**TRADITION:** West African

**HOME:** Varies; often homeless

**ALSO KNOWN AS:** Legba (Haitian vodou)

Eshu, the Yoruba god of chance and uncertainty, can be a real pain. Officially, his job is to carry information between the people of Earth and the Great God in heaven, and he is well suited for it. He knows how to speak every language, and he's sly enough to be very convincing.

Unofficially, he is an incorrigible prankster, a mischievous spirit of chaos who haunts crossroads and marketplaces and plays cruel tricks on passersby. He creates conflict wherever he goes, stealing, lying, destroying, and turning people against each other.

## HOW ESHU GOT HIS JOB

Long ago, the supreme creator god lived with us on Earth. One day, Eshu came to the Great God with a warning: Some thieves were planning to rob his garden. The Great God thanked him and sent him on his way.

That night, while everyone slept, Eshu returned in secret. He crept into the Great God's house and borrowed his sandals. Then he sneaked around back and, while wearing the sandals, dug up all the yams in the garden. He returned the sandals, but kept the yams.

Early the next morning, Eshu yelled for everyone to come see what had happened. The Great God's yams had been stolen—but the thief had left footprints! The Great God summoned everyone in town to the garden. One by one, they tested their feet against the prints, and one by one, they were all proven innocent. The prints were enormous, far bigger than any normal person's feet. But perhaps, suggested Eshu, they might fit a god's feet? The Great God scoffed, but sure enough, his feet matched.

Many stories pair Eshu with Ifa, a god of order. In one story, Eshu tricks Ifa into revealing the secret of predicting the future—a secret that was later passed on to humans.

The Great God erupted in anger. He insisted he was innocent and that Eshu had tricked him. Then he packed up his things and left—not to his home, but up to the heavens, far away from everyone on Earth. As a punishment, he forced Eshu to travel to heaven once every day to tell him everything that happened down below on Earth, and that's been Eshu's job ever since.

## ESHU RUINS EVERYONE'S DAY

Once, there were two farmers who were best friends. They lived next door to each other, and they spent nearly every free moment together. They even dressed alike. They were happy and healthy and content, until Eshu decided to mess with them.

He stuck a pipe to the back of his head and dangled a club over his shoulder so it looked like it was hanging down his back. Then he put on a hat that was half-white and half-black and went for a walk along the border separating the friends' farms, making sure that both of them saw him.

The next time the farmers talked, they mentioned the man who had walked between them. One said the man was wearing a white hat, but the other said it was black. One said he was walking forward, but the other swore he was walking backward. Both were furious that the other would lie. Soon their argument turned into a shouting match, and then a fight so big that the king was called to intervene.

When the farmers were brought before him, both accused the other of lying. That was when Eshu arrived, laughing at his own prank. He announced that the fools were both telling the truth and explained his trick to the crowd. No one was amused, least of all the king. But Eshu was quick—before the king's guards could catch him, he ran out to the village and set all of the houses on fire.

It was pandemonium. Everyone ran from their huts, carrying bundles of their possessions. As each one exited, Eshu ran up and offered to keep their stuff safe while they escaped the inferno. Then he took all the bundles and handed them out as gifts to whatever random people he came across. By the end of the day, the village was in ruins, its people and their stuff scattered in all directions.

# FREYA

## THE LOVELY ENCHANTRESS

# FREYA

**TRADITION:** Norse

**HOME:** Vanaheim, sometimes Asgard

**ALSO KNOWN AS:** Frija (German)

**W**hether you are a Viking in love or in love with a Viking, you can't go wrong with Freya. She's the most beautiful goddess in the Norse pantheon, associated with love, beauty, fertility, and fancy things of all kinds. Her realm, Folkvangr, is full of gorgeous, leafy fields, and some say she brings half the warriors who die in battle to live with her there. She tends the gods' fruit trees and collects their life-giving fruit. Without that fruit, the gods would grow old and die. She's always well dressed in a magical falcon-feather cloak and a dwarf-forged necklace. She also has powerful magic—she's the one who taught the gods *seidr*.

## WHAT'S SEIDR?

Seidr is a kind of old Norse magic. It was practiced in Viking times by women called *völvas* who traveled from town to town and sold their services to the locals, advising, healing, blessing, and predicting the future. If they chose, they could also lay down some serious curses. It's no wonder the völva was both admired and feared.

Men could also practice seidr, technically. But it was considered super unmanly, so not many did.

> I CAN TEACH YOU TO REWEAVE FATE ITSELF.

> PFFFF, THAT'S WOMEN'S WORK!

## FREYA AND FRIGG

Freya has a lot in common with another Norse goddess: Frigg. They are both wise, both women, and both excellent at magic. *Freya* even sounds a little bit like *Frigg*, and the name of Freya's husband, Odr, sounds a little like the name of Frigg's husband, Odin (see his chapter on page 176). Even more confusing, Freya and Frigg seem to share a number of the same stories.

There's a theory that, at one point, they might have been the same goddess. A few centuries before either showed up, people in central Europe worshipped another wise magic goddess named Frija, wife of Wodan (a predecessor to Odin). The theory is that, as the Norse religion evolved, Frija began to split into Freya and Frigg. But religions change slowly, and before the split was complete, Christianity displaced Norse paganism in most of Scandinavia. And since most of our sources come from around that time, what we have is a snapshot of a goddess split in progress.

It's not exactly clear which, but either Freya or Frigg is the namesake of *Friday*.

# FREYR

LORD OF PEACE

# FREYR

**TRADITION:** Norse
**HOME:** Alfheim
**ALSO KNOWN AS:** Frey, Yngvi

Popular depictions of Viking gods are full of war and violence. But if you think Norse mythology is only giants meeting the business ends of hammers, axes, and spears, think again. Mythologies reflect the societies that create them, and societies can't get by on violence alone. They need food, for instance. They need crops and livestock and money and supplies, and periods of peace long enough to do something with them. That's where Freyr comes in.

Freyr is a god of fertility, wealth, and peace. He was one of the most popular Viking gods, and it's easy to see why. His priests would travel far and wide, pulling a cart with a statue of him from town to town. When they arrived in a village, they threw huge, days-long parties, celebrating Freyr and blessing the village and inviting everyone to join in. In between eating, drinking, and carrying on, partygoers would approach the statue and pray for big families, good harvests, and solutions to their problems.

Despite his popularity in Viking times, we don't have many good sources on Freyr, and those we do have leave a lot of gaps. One of the few stories we do (sort of) know is the tale of Freyr and Gerd.

## FREYR WOOS/THREATENS A LADY

One of Odin's greatest treasures was his throne, from which one could see what was going on anywhere in the world. It was from this throne that Freyr first saw Gerd, the most beautiful of all the giants. It was love at first sight.

The thing was, Gerd lived far away, in a land owned by the giants. And giants didn't take too kindly to gods like Freyr. There was no way Freyr could get to her himself, so he found a hero, Skírnir, to go in his stead. He gave Skírnir a magic sword in exchange for a promise that Skírnir would find Gerd and bring her back.

### Aesir, Vanir, and the Aesir-Vanir War

There are two groups of Norse gods, and they haven't always gotten along. Most of the Norse gods in this book are of the Aesir, who make their home in Asgard, at the highest reaches of the world tree. Odin, Thor, Frigg, Loki, and Baldr are among their number. Freyr and Freya, on the other hand, are members of another tribe, called the Vanir. In most stories, the two tribes get along well enough that it can be hard to tell for sure which is which. But there was one time when they didn't.

It began when Freya arrived in Asgard, offering to help the gods with her magic. The Aesir eagerly accepted. No matter how big or outlandish their requests, Freya fulfilled them. But as their wishes were granted, the Aesir became selfish, and it wasn't long before that selfishness led them to fight with each other.

Freya was to blame—or at least, that's what they told her when they decided to kill her. They tried three times to burn her at the stake, but each time she stepped from the ashes unharmed.

OH NO, NOT EVEN **MORE** FIRE. WHATEVER WILL I DO?

Freya's friends and family among the Vanir came to help, and the whole thing spiraled out of control until the two sides were at war. They fought each other to a stalemate that lasted for ages, with countless injuries but no end in sight. Eventually, exhausted, they arranged a truce. They all agreed to go back home and stop trying to kill each other. But to keep each other honest, they exchanged hostages: the Aesir gods Hoenir and Mimir went to live with the Vanir, and the Vanir gods Freyr, Freya, and Njord went to live with the Aesir.

Skírnir trekked across the world, over mountains, across rivers, and past frigid plains, until he found Gerd in the great hall of Gymir. He entered in triumph and told Gerd about Freyr and asked her to come back with him. Gerd said no.

Skírnir told her that if she married Freyr, she could have some of the golden apples that gave the gods eternal youth. Gerd said no. Skírnir offered her Odin's magical ring, which produced eight more golden rings every ninth night. Gerd still said no. He threatened to kill her, but Gerd was unmoved. He threatened to kill her father, and she still refused. Finally, he warned her that if she kept refusing, he would leave, but she would be hearing from the gods Odin and Loki. At that, Gerd relented and agreed to meet with Freyr a few days later. And that's how Freyr and Gerd wound up together.

> Freyr is known as the lord of the elves, who in Norse mythology are bright, beautiful, and sometimes (but not always) nice.

# GAIA

## THE EARTH

## GAIA

**TRADITION:** Greek/Roman
**HOME:** We live on her
**ALSO KNOWN AS:** Gaea, Terra (Roman)

Gaia is one of the oldest Greek goddesses. Her origins are unknown, but probably prehistoric, and certainly predate the most famous Greek gods of Mount Olympus. She is also old within her mythology, born at the dawn of time, the earth itself in goddess form. She's caring, though she has a temper, especially where her children are concerned. As the mother of more or less everyone, protecting one child often means fighting with another.

## THE ORIGINS OF EVERYTHING

Long, long ago, there was nothing—no Earth, no sky, just an endless, formless void. From that void emerged the first, primordial gods, each of whom embodied a basic part of creation. There was Gaia, the earth; Tartarus, the world beneath; Erebus, the gloom of the underworld; Eros, love itself; and Nyx, the sinister darkness. Gaia created Ouranos, the sky, and together Gaia and Ouranos produced many, many others.

Their first kids were the three Hecatonchires (the Hundred-Armed), enormous, terrifying monsters with fifty heads and a hundred arms each. Next they had the first three Cyclopes, strong, one-eyed giants.

Gaia loved her children, but Ouranos hated them and buried them beneath the earth. However, because Gaia *was* the earth, that really meant he buried them inside Gaia. She missed her kids, and holding them inside her caused serious pain, which is why Gaia decided that Ouranos had to go.

## GAIA PUNISHES HER FIRST KID

Gaia and Ouranos's next kids were some of the most famous in all of Greek mythology: the twelve Titans. Six male and six female, all very powerful. One by one, Gaia asked her sons to help her overthrow their father, and one by one, they refused—all except Kronos, the youngest.

Gaia made Kronos a supernaturally strong sickle and helped him prepare an ambush. That night, when Ouranos came down to get cuddly with Gaia, Kronos burst out and vanquished his father. That done, Kronos settled into his new role as king of the gods. But despite Gaia's pleas, he refused to release the Hecatonchires or the Cyclopes, which is why Gaia decided that Kronos also had to go.

## GAIA PUNISHES HER NEXT KIDS

Around this time, Kronos heard a prophecy that he would be overthrown by one of his kids. So every time his wife, Rhea, gave birth, Kronos ate the baby just to be safe. Gaia offered to help Rhea save her children. When her next son, Zeus, was born, Gaia sneaked him away to safety. In Zeus's place, Rhea fed Kronos a well-disguised rock.

When Zeus grew up, he released the Hecatonchires and the Cyclopes and with their help overthrew Kronos and the other Titans. He freed his brothers and sisters from Kronos's stomach and established a new kingdom of the gods on Mount Olympus. But in the aftermath, despite Gaia's objections, Zeus imprisoned the Titans—which is why Gaia decided that Zeus, too, had to go.

THIS "DECOY" IS A ROCK.

JUST TELL HIM IT'S A GOD OF STONES.

## GAIA TRIES TO PUNISH MORE KIDS

Gaia created some new kids, the Gigantes, who she thought were big and mean enough to overthrow the gods of Olympus. She thought wrong. Zeus, along with his brothers, sisters, and children, fought the giants to a standstill. But while they could injure the giants, a prophecy said that only a mortal could land a killing blow. So Athena went out and fetched the hero Heracles, and the giants were defeated.

Enraged, Gaia created an even bigger, more awful monster, Typhoeus, who had a hundred different heads, hundreds of hands, and enormous snakes for legs. Zeus faced the monster in single combat, and after a close and costly battle, drove it from Greece and crushed it beneath a volcano.

At last, Gaia backed off and made peace with Zeus.

# GANESHA

## THE REMOVER OF OBSTACLES

# GANESHA

**TRADITION:** Indian/Hindu
**HOME:** Mount Kailash
**ALSO KNOWN AS:** Ganesh, Ganapati

Ganesha is one of the most popular Hindu gods, and it's easy to see why. He is rich, generous, good-natured, and happy to help anyone in need as long as they aren't jerks about it. He's a god of wisdom, commerce, and beginnings. He has a sly wit, but he's never cruel—although he can be a bit greedy, especially where sweets are concerned.

His most famous role is as the remover of obstacles, clearing away things that might block success. Homework assignments, business deals, and even personal hobbies will always go smoothly if Ganesha's helping them along.

## THE BIRTH OF GANESHA

There are several versions of Ganesha's birth story. This is one of the more popular versions:

The goddess Parvati spent a lot of time by herself. She lived with her husband, Shiva, but he often left her alone when he traveled on god business. One day, she decided to create a new god to protect her and keep her company. She molded some mud into a person and used her powers to imbue it with life.

When Shiva returned and went to see his beloved wife, he found himself blocked by some "guard" he had never met. Shiva was enraged, so he chopped off the guard's head. And that's when Parvati walked out to see what was the matter. She took one look and screamed, cursing Shiva for killing her son.

Now that he understood the situation, Shiva rushed to make it right. He left at once and returned with the head of an elephant, the wisest animal, and attached it to the dead boy's neck. And just like that, the boy came back to life: a wise, potbellied, elephant-headed baby, who grew up to be Ganesha.

OH MY BABY... MY BABY...

IT'S OK! IT'S OK! SEE? GOOD AS NEW!

## THE EXPLOSION OF GANESHA

If Ganesha has one weakness, it's sweets. Fruit, candy, cakes, pastries—if it's sugary and delicious, Ganesha wants to eat it. Occasionally, though, his appetite gets him into trouble.

One day, Ganesha ate a whole lot of cakes. He ate until he was full and then kept on eating until he got such a horrible stomachache that he had no choice but to stop for a while. In the meantime he went out for a ride on his mouse, Mushika, hoping it would help him digest.

He hadn't gotten far when the mouse saw a huge snake and jumped in fear, sending Ganesha flying. He landed right on his cake-strained stomach, and it exploded. Cakes flew everywhere. But Ganesha, always calm, simply collected the cakes and stuffed them back into his stomach. Then he grabbed the snake that had startled his mouse and used it to tie himself shut.

## The Gods and Their Vahanas

A Vahana is the mythical mount of a Hindu god. They are usually animals, and gods are often depicted riding them in religious art. Here are just a few of the more famous ones:

| GOD | VAHANA |
|-----|--------|
| Ganesha | Mushika, the giant mouse |
| Indra | Uchchaihshravas, the seven-headed flying horse |
| Kartikeya (Ganesha's war-god brother) | Parvani, the peacock |
| Kubera (a portly god of wealth) | Nara, which means *man* |
| Parvati/Durga | Dawon, the tiger and/or lion (sources vary) |
| Shiva | Nandi, the huge white bull |
| Vishnu | Garuda, the bird-person |

## How We Know What We Know About Hindu Mythology

If you want to study Hindu mythology, you're in luck! Compared to most myths, those from India are extremely well documented, with sources going back thousands of years. But with so many sources from so many different eras, it can be tough to know what to make of it all. Here are a few of the major ones:

- **The Vedas:** The earliest written accounts of Indian religion are also some of the oldest writings, period, dating from around 1000 BCE. Their hymns and mantras allude to a lot of ancient myths.

- **The Mahabharata:** One of the two greatest Hindu epics, and the longest poem ever written. It tells the story of an ancient Indian war and includes some great stories about various gods, along with a big helping of religious lessons.

- **The Ramayana:** The other of the two greatest Hindu epics, which tells the story of the life of Rama and his wars against the demon king Ravana.

- **The Puranas:** A catch-all term for a variety of ancient literature aside from the sources above. They cover all sorts of topics, including myths, legends, and folktales.

As he finished fastening his new snake belt, he heard laughter. He turned around to find that the moon and its wives, the constellations, were cracking up at the whole thing. So Ganesha, always calm, broke off one of his tusks and threw it right at the moon's stupid face.

The impact turned the moon black. Without its light, the nights became so dangerous that folks were afraid to leave their homes. They begged the gods to bring the light back, and the gods asked Ganesha to forgive the moon. Ganesha did—but only partly, which is why the moon is still dark sometimes.

Another myth says that Ganesha lost his tusk because he snapped it off and used it to write the *Mahabharata*, one of the great epic poems of Hinduism.

# GIANTS

## AND OTHER PEOPLE OF UNUSUAL SIZE

All kinds of mythologies feature giants. Some are just another sort of god, a power for good or ill. Some are creatures of chaos, trying to devour the world. Some are monsters that battle heroes. They show up in a ton of creation myths, sometimes as the creator of the world and sometimes as a planet-sized corpse the world is created from. These are a few famous giants:

## BALOR OF THE EVIL EYE

According to Celtic mythology, before humans lived in Ireland, it was home to a race of gods called the Tuatha Dé Danann. But before *they* lived in Ireland, it was home to a nation of giants called the Fomorians. The biggest, baddest Fomorian was their king, Balor, a giant with one eye, whose gaze alone could destroy whole armies.

When the Tuatha Dé Danann first invaded, Balor heard a prophecy that his own grandson would defeat him. He attempted to prevent that by imprisoning his daughter—if she couldn't meet anyone, she couldn't get pregnant and he couldn't have any grandkids.

Unfortunately for him, one of the Tuatha Dé Danann managed to sneak in to see Balor's daughter, and the two produced a beautiful baby god named Lugh. Years later, Lugh shot Balor with a sling, knocking his evil eye so far back in his head that its power was turned back on the Fomorian army, destroying them all.

BOO.

## GRENDEL

*Beowulf*, the Old English poem in which the mysterious enemy Grendel and his mother appear, doesn't say much about their appearance. Instead, it describes the way they skulked at night, attacking warriors and devouring them whole. A good thing, then, that Beowulf killed them both.

## HUMBABA

Humbaba appears in the Sumerian *Epic of Gilgamesh*. He is a ferocious giant with a lion's head, fiery breath, and a body covered in spikes. Gilgamesh tracked him to his forest hideout and tricked him into trading away his power. Then Gilgamesh sucker punched him, knocked him out, and took him prisoner. Humbaba begged for his life, and Gilgamesh might have let him go, but his wild-man buddy Enkidu convinced him that Humbaba was far too dangerous to trust. So, they chopped off his head instead.

## KUNG LO

A Vietnamese myth says the whole world was created by a giant named Kung Lo. He used his head to lift the sky up off the earth. Then he dug up a bunch of soil and rocks and molded them into a pillar, and used that pillar to keep the sky propped up. Once the sky was stable, he broke the pillar up and threw the pieces all around. They crashed to Earth and became mountains and islands.

## PAN GU

One of the oldest creation stories in China says that long ago, the universe was a swirling black ball of chaos. The chaos hardened itself into an egg, and inside that egg grew the giant Pan Gu. He slept for thousands of years, and when he finally woke up, he broke open the egg, pushing the top up and the bottom down. In the process, he split up the earth and the sky. The longer he held them apart, the larger he became, and the larger he became, the farther he pushed them apart. When Pan Gu died, thousands of years later, he was enormous, and his body became the features of the earth as we know it today.

## POLYPHEMUS

Polyphemus was one of the cyclopes, a race of Greek giants with one big eye in the middle of their heads. On his voyage home from the Trojan War, the hero Odysseus stopped on Polyphemus's island with some of his men. Polyphemus captured them, ate two, and imprisoned the rest in his cave with a herd of sheep. Odysseus knew that if he stayed there, he and his men would be eaten. But he also knew he couldn't hope to win a fight against the giant. So he found another way out.

First he offered Polyphemus wine, chatting with him and refilling his cup until the giant was so drunk that he fell asleep. Then Odysseus and his men sharpened the cyclops's club into a hard point and used it to poke out his eye. Polyphemus roared in pain and vowed revenge. He might not have been able to see, but he stood guard at the mouth of his cave to catch his prisoners as they tried to escape. However, cunning Odysseus had a plan for this, too: He and his men tied themselves to the undersides of Polyphemus's sheep. When the sheep wandered out of the cave to graze, Polyphemus couldn't feel the men tied underneath, and they escaped (mostly) unharmed.

## PURUSHA

An Indian myth says the first creature in all of creation was Purusha, a huge giant with a thousand heads, a thousand eyes, and a thousand feet. The first gods and sages emerged from Purusha and decided to sacrifice him in order to create the world. They tied him down and built a fire, burning their offerings of oil, grain, and butter. Then they cut Purusha into little pieces and used those pieces to create the world. His feet became the earth, his head became the sky, and his belly button became the air in between. His soul was transformed into the moon, and his eyes into the sun. From his mouth came Indra, king of the gods, and Agni, the god of the sacrificial fire. His breath became Vayu, the wind god. Finally, the first people emerged: priests from his mouth, warriors from his arms, farmers from his thighs, and lowly servants from his feet.

## SVYATOGOR

A Russian legend tells of a knight who was so huge that when he rode his horse, his helmet split the clouds. He had been a great warrior once, but that was long ago—now he was wrinkled and old.

One day he was attacked by a normal-sized knight named Ilya Muromets. Muromets charged Svyatogor, bashing him with his mace as hard as he could, but Svyatogor was so huge that he hardly even noticed. When it became clear that Muromets wouldn't give up, Svyatogor picked him up off the ground and stuck him in his massive pocket. Eventually they got to talking and became friends.

Some time later, the two came upon an enormous stone coffin and felt a strange desire to lie in it. Muromets climbed in first, but he was too small to fill it, so he got out. When Svyatogor climbed inside, it fit him perfectly, and the lid slammed shut. No matter what the two knights did, they couldn't get the coffin open. Finally, seeing the hopelessness of his situation, Svyatogor accepted his death. He asked only that Muromets tie the giant's horse to a nearby tree, so that the two might die together.

## TYPHOEUS

Typhoeus, sometimes called Typhus, is an ancient beast of Greek mythology. He is shaped like a man with snakes instead of legs and stands so tall that his heads brush the stars. That's *heads*, plural—while most gods have one head, he has a hundred, each from a different animal. He's imprisoned in Tartarus, the maximum-security prison beneath the underworld, as punishment for attacking the gods of Olympus. But even from down there, he sometimes causes problems—hurricanes are said to be his work.

## YMIR

The original Norse giant Ymir is the ancestor of most Norse gods as well as the gods' mortal enemies, the frost giants. He was killed long ago by the god Odin and his brothers, Vili and Ve, and they used his body in an ancient act of creation. His flowing blood became the oceans and lakes, and his bones the mountains and rocks. His hair became trees, his brains the clouds, and the dome of his skull the sky.

## ZIPACNA

Zipacna was one of a trio of Mayan giants whom the gods vanquished with the help of the hero twins Xbalanque and Hunahpu. The twins tracked Zipacna to his stomping grounds and prepared a trap in a nearby ravine. They surrounded a huge boulder with flowers so that it looked like a giant crab, and then they waited.

When Zipacna finally happened by, they asked him what he was doing, and he told them he was looking for food. When they mentioned the giant crab and pointed the way, he excitedly ran for it. But the boulder had been placed at such an angle that the moment Zipacna touched it, it rolled on top of him. He managed to wriggle his way free, but in the process he either broke his neck or choked to death.

CRAB

# GILGAMESH

## GOD-KING OF URUK

# GILGAMESH

**TRADITION**: Sumerian/Mesopotamian
**HOME**: The city of Uruk
**ALSO KNOWN AS**: Bilgamesh

At more than five thousand years old, the *Epic of Gilgamesh* is the earliest work of literature we can still read—that is, the earliest work that hasn't been burned, broken, pillaged, or misplaced over the centuries. The most complete version of the story we have (on a dozen cracked clay tablets) was written in Babylonia and based on even older Sumerian poems about a legendary king named Gilgamesh.

## THE *EPIC OF GILGAMESH*

Gilgamesh was the part-human, part-god king of Uruk, an ancient city in modern-day Iraq, and like many kings of the ancient world, he was kind of a jerk. He abused his kingly power, forcing folks to build his buildings, fight his wars, till his fields, and sometimes even hang out with him in his palace. The people of Uruk hated him. They prayed to the gods to send someone, anyone, who could help them against Gilgamesh. The gods answered their prayers. They took some clay and molded it into a ferocious wild man called Enkidu.

GILGAMESH                    ENKIDU

## Country Gods and City Gods

For most of human history, people lived in small groups, limited by the amount of food they could hunt or gather. And while some groups eventually learned to farm and built towns and cities, others didn't, continuing to hunt and gather and raid settled areas and take stuff. You can see the differences in their mythologies. A nomadic people's most important gods were often focused on the sky, nature, animals, and warriors—all things central to their lives. As societies became more urban, their gods changed with them: hunting gods gave way to farming gods and were joined by gods of crafts, commerce, and government. Some myths even seem to reflect this change—for instance, the city king Gilgamesh vs. the wild man Enkidu.

While Gilgamesh was a cultured warrior-king, Enkidu was a hair-covered savage who lived with animals. He was uncivilized, and his wildness gave him enough power to defeat Gilgamesh—or would have, if he hadn't first encountered a priestess who showed him human civilization. Enkidu started hanging out in towns, learned some skills, and at one point even got a job. By the time he got around to fighting Gilgamesh, he had become too civilized to defeat him. After their fight, they spent a night talking, and by the morning they were best friends. From then on, Gilgamesh and Enkidu traveled the world together, doing great deeds and slaying great foes, including the Humbaba. But it couldn't last.

One day Ishtar, goddess of love and war, demanded that Gilgamesh be her new lover. Gilgamesh had heard about the awful things Ishtar had done to her past lovers and wisely refused. This enraged Ishtar so much that she unleashed the Bull of Heaven, a huge, ravenous beast that caused droughts and famines and earthquakes. Gilgamesh and Enkidu managed to cut the bull in half, and when Ishtar complained, Enkidu threw its butt at her.

But the Bull of Heaven was owned by the gods, and the gods didn't like it when people killed their stuff. They punished Enkidu by infecting him with a disease, and soon he was dead.

Gilgamesh had never really thought about death. But as he mourned his friend, he realized that he didn't want to die. So he journeyed across the ocean to ask the world's only immortal guy, Utnapishtim, how to get eternal life.

## UTNAPISHTIM'S ARK

Utnapishtim told Gilgamesh his story. Long ago, the gods got angry and decided to drown the world with a flood. Before it hit, one god came to Utnapishtim and instructed him to build a huge boat and load it with his family and all the animals he could find. Utnapishtim did as he was told, and watched from the boat as the water rose and the whole world was washed away. After a week, the flood began to recede, leaving the boat lodged on a mountain. Utnapishtim released a dove, a swallow, and a raven. The dove and the swallow returned, but the raven didn't—which meant the raven had found dry land. So Utnapishtim opened his boat and let everyone out. The gods rewarded him and his wife with eternal life.

Gilgamesh didn't have any floods or boats or favors from the gods, so Utnapishtim's tale wasn't much help. But as he was leaving, Utnapishtim mentioned a plant that could restore a man's youth. Gilgamesh found the plant, but before he could use it, a snake ate it up and learned to shed its skin. So Gilgamesh went home and accepted that death would come for him just like everyone else.

### If This Sounds Familiar . . .

If you've ever read the Bible's book of Genesis, Gilgamesh's story might sound familiar. Take Enkidu: a man created from dirt, who lives with animals and nature, until a woman tempts him with knowledge of civilization—sort of like Adam and Eve. Or Utnapishtim: After a warning from a god, he builds a boat and loads it with animals, survives a flood, and checks for land with birds—just like the story of Noah's ark.

The *Epic of Gilgamesh* and the stories in the Bible all come from the same general region in the Middle East. We can't say for sure whether one was directly inspired by the other, but it's likely that versions of these stories were floating around long before either was written down.

# HADES

LORD OF THE UNDERWORLD

## HADES

**TRADITION:** Greek/Roman
**HOME:** Hades (the place)
**ALSO KNOWN AS:** Aïdes, Pluto (Roman)

Given how important death and the afterlife are to many religions, it's interesting that the underworld is rarely mentioned in Greek myth. It mostly comes up when a living person decides to visit. The same is true of its king, Hades, who shows up more often in modern stories than he ever did in mythology.

Hades is a dark, serious, gloomy god, but relentless as death. While he is technically allowed up on Mount Olympus, he usually stays down below, far from the worlds of men and gods. He also holds sway over the rest of the underground and the precious metals hiding down there—which is why he is sometimes called Pluto (*giver of wealth*).

## HADES IN HADES

The Greek underworld is also called Hades, and it's as dark and dreary as its namesake. You won't find skeletons or corpses here—just the god Hades; his wife, Persephone; their monstrous three-headed dog, Cerberus; and countless drifting spirits.

Early myths placed Hades beyond the western ocean, but as the Greeks learned more about the geography of the world, they shifted its location to somewhere deep underground. The only ways in or out were through caves and underground rivers, including the Styx (river of hate), Acheron (river of woe), Lethe (river of forgetfulness), Cocytus (river of wailing), and Phlegethon (river of fire).

## HADES AND PERSEPHONE

Hades' wife, Persephone, wasn't a willing bride so much as the victim of a violent kidnapping. She was happily picking flowers when, all of a sudden, Hades burst from the ground, grabbed her, and pulled her down into the underworld.

## Dying While Greek

Ancient Greeks believed that when you died your psyche would leave and float away. But a psyche isn't like a soul. *Psyche*, in Greek, means "breath," and when your body stops breathing, your psyche becomes an echo, a shadow, a ghost, an *eidolon* ("phantom image"). An eidolon has no thoughts or sensations or consciousness. It just drifts on down through the gates of Hades and waits with the rest of the dead.

Later Greeks added some punishments and rewards to their vision of the afterlife. The truly wicked faced ingeniously awful punishments. Sisyphus had to push a boulder up a hill, but never quite got there before it rolled back down, while Tantalus spent eternity hungry and thirsty, with food and water always just out of reach. Great heroes, on the other hand, got to live out their post-lives in the beautiful fields of Elysium. But these extreme fates were reserved for the very best and worst people. If you haven't impressed or annoyed any Greek gods, it's normal, boring Hades for you.

Persephone's mother, the harvest goddess Demeter, heard her scream, but before she could find her daughter the ground had closed up, leaving no trace. She searched everywhere, asking everyone if they had seen what happened to Persephone. It was Helios, the sun god, who broke the news: Zeus had told Hades he could marry Persephone, and neither of them bothered to ask what Persephone thought about it. But Helios told her not to worry, because Hades was so rich and powerful that he would make a great husband.

Needless to say, Demeter was not consoled. She fell into a depression, stopped caring for herself, and took to wandering the world disguised as a sad old woman. But she was the goddess of the harvest, and while she neglected her duties, plants died, and people who ate plants died. Since dead people can't worship the gods, Zeus decided to do something.

> Hades owned a magic helmet that could make its wearer invisible. It found its way into the hands of several great heroes over the years, including Perseus.

He sent Hermes, the messenger of the gods, down to the underworld to ask for Persephone back, and Hades was surprisingly fine with it. He told Persephone she was free to go, but hoped that, someday, she would change her mind. And, in the meantime, if anyone ever insulted her, he would make sure they "atoned" for it in the afterlife. But then, as Persephone turned to leave, Hades stuck a pomegranate seed in her mouth, which she swallowed.

When Persephone got to her mom's place, they both rejoiced. Then her mom asked if she had eaten anything in the underworld. Persephone admitted that she had, and a newly distraught Demeter revealed that eating underworld food binds you there. Persephone would have to spend a third of every year with Hades, in Hades, forever. But still, Demeter had her daughter back, so she let the plants grow again—for part of every year, at least.

# HATHOR

## THE EYE OF RA

# HATHOR

**TRADITION:** Egyptian
**HOME:** The heavens
**ALSO KNOWN AS:** The Eye of Ra

Ancient Egypt had plenty of gods and goddesses, but it can sometimes be hard to tell them apart. It's not that they have that much in common (although some do) or that they look the same (although, again, some do). It's just that there are dozens of similar but different mythologies that developed in several different cities over thousands and thousands of years. Sometimes a god gradually replaced another, absorbing some of their qualities and leaving the rest. Sometimes several gods came to be considered one god with a bunch of different names. In Hathor's case, both happened.

Hathor is a goddess of love and joy, life and death, and women. She's kind and generous, and in her role as the Eye of Ra, extremely powerful. She helps women in childbirth and protects their children from harm. Years later, when they die, she's there to help them through the trials of the underworld.

For a time, Hathor was the most popular goddess in Egypt. Scholars think she probably evolved from an ancient, powerful mother goddess who was worshipped long before records were kept. As Hathor gained worshippers, she became linked to many other goddesses, including Sekhmet, Bastet, and Mut. Depending on the myth, she might be the mother, wife, and/or daughter of various sun gods, as well as the source of their power. But as time passed, Hathor's fortunes changed, and she wound up largely replaced by a relative newcomer named Isis.

I SPY WITH MY LITTLE EYE...

## THE EYE OF RA

An eye, in Egyptian mythology, isn't just a body part—it's also a metaphor. In the ancient Egyptian language, the word for *eye* sounded a lot like the word for "to do," which might be why it's associated with the divine power to do things. The Eye of Ra was often described as a goddess in her own right, a female counterpart to the god Ra.

If Ra is the sun, the Eye is its brightness, its heat, and its life-giving energy. If the Eye is injured, Ra is crippled. If she gets upset and leaves him, his own power has left him—though given time, he can create a new Eye. Many goddesses have been considered the Eye of Ra, but Hathor is one of the most common.

## THE DISTANT GODDESS

This myth shows up in different forms all across ancient Egypt. In this version, the Eye of Ra is Hathor. For one reason or another, the Eye of Ra got really upset with Ra and left him. She turned herself into a wild cat and lived in the desert, far away from the settled lands of Egypt.

Ra was powerless without Hathor. He asked another god to go look for her and bring her home. After a long search, the god found her, and after much talking and cajoling, convinced her to come back. Once they returned, the Eye reunited with the sun god and together they created a divine child, who would become the new sun god.

HEEEERRE, KITTY KITTY KITTY KITTY...

# HEIMDALL

## THE KEEN WATCHMAN

# HEIMDALL

**TRADITION:** Norse
**HOME:** Himinbjörg
**ALSO KNOWN AS:** Heimdallr

Heimdall is something of a mystery in Norse mythology. He was clearly important in his time, but we don't have enough sources to say exactly how or why. We know that he's the watchman of the gods and stands guard at Himinbjörg, watching over Bifröst, the rainbow bridge that connects the home of the gods, Asgard, to the other realms. We know he's amazingly perceptive, with eyes that can see for hundreds of miles and ears so keen they can hear grass growing. We know he's so vigilant that he hardly ever sleeps, and even then only for a moment. But we don't know what his personality is like, what the Vikings thought of him, or what stories he might be involved in.

We do have a few tantalizing clues. There is evidence he might have been associated with rams, for example. A few old poems refer to swords as *Heimdall's head*, which might imply a head-sword story we've long since lost. And we have references to a poem about Heimdall called the "Heimdallargaldr" that might answer all our questions, if only any copies still existed.

CLANG

We do, however, know how Heimdall will die. When Ragnarok, the battle to end the world, begins, Heimdall will see the frost giants preparing to assault the gates of Asgard. He will blow his horn, the Gjallarhorn, to warn the gods of the attack. And then, as the battle rages and the world ends, he and Loki will face off in single combat, and they will each be slain by the other's weapon.

## RIG'S TRAVELS

While we don't have any stories that are definitely about Heimdall, we do have one that might be about him. Rig, the hero of an old Norse poem, has been identified with Heimdall.

The poem describes Rig/Heimdall wandering around and visiting the families of a slave, a farmer, and a noble. He spends a night at each of their houses and sleeps in bed with them, between the husband and wife. Nine months later, each couple has a kid. The first grows into a rough peasant slave, the second into a hardworking free man, and the last into a noble who leads them all. Some scholars use this story to argue that Heimdall might have been the creator of humans, but without more evidence, it's hard to say.

According to some sources, Heimdall had a whopping nine separate mothers!

HRRRRRNNNNNNK!!

## How We Know What We Know About Norse Mythology

Unfortunately, we don't have many sources on Norse mythology. Ancient Norsemen didn't write much of it down. Most of the folks who did write it down lived after Christianity replaced the old religions of Scandinavia, and even their writing is largely lost to time. Here is some of what we do have:

- **The Poetic Edda:** A collection of traditional poems about Norse gods. No one is sure who wrote them or when—probably various people between the eighth and thirteenth centuries.

- **The Prose Edda:** A book about Norse mythology that was written by Snorri Sturluson, a rich, powerful guy in thirteenth-century Iceland. Some of it is based on sources we still have, some of it is based on sources that we don't have, and some of it was totally made up by Mr. Sturluson. The problem is, we aren't 100 percent sure which is which.

- **Sagas and histories:** For medieval scholars, history and mythology weren't strictly separate things. A lot of documents from the era mix folktales, mythology, and things that actually happened. A number of royal families, for instance, traced their ancestry back to mythological events.

- **Comparative mythology:** Norse mythology has a lot in common with mythology from central Europe. Sometimes comparing the two can lead to interesting insights.

- **Archeology:** Going through ancient people's stuff can tell us a lot about them.

...AND LOKI SPEAKETH, "I KNOW THOU ART, BUT WHAT AM I?"

# HERA

## THE QUEEN OF THE GODS

# HERA

**TRADITION:** Greek/Roman
**HOME:** Mount Olympus
**ALSO KNOWN AS:** Juno (Roman)

She is married to Zeus, and he isn't exactly the most faithful husband. Hera's a kind goddess of marriage, women, and the sky, and she can be a powerful patron if you get on her good side. But she's also stubborn, jealous, and fond of revenge.

Hera doesn't take revenge on Zeus—or at least, not directly. She tried once, but Zeus found out what she was planning and punished her, hanging her by her wrists for days with anchors tied to her ankles. So now she pays her suffering forward, taking revenge on the women Zeus seduces, and often on their children as well.

Before you judge Hera, remember that gods tend to reflect the cultures that worship them. In ancient Greece, as in many societies, men had a lot more power than women. Little wonder that the king of the gods has more power than his queen—or that Hera, goddess of marriage, does what she can to defend hers.

## HERA TAKES REVENGE ON SEMELE

One of Zeus's many mistresses was a princess of Thebes named Semele. Zeus, perhaps hoping to keep his trysts under wraps, disguised himself as a human before every visit. For a time, they were happy. Semele even got pregnant. But then Hera found out and decided to punish them both.

SO... ARE YOU SEEING ANYONE?

She disguised herself as a little old woman and slowly made friends with Semele. It took a while, but eventually Semele started talking about the incredible guy she was dating. Hera revealed that Semele's boyfriend wasn't just some guy—he was the king of the gods, Zeus. She told Semele that if she waited until Zeus was in bed with her, he would probably grant any wish she asked for.

Later, when Semele and Zeus were in bed, Semele asked him for a wish, and Zeus promised to grant her anything. Just as Hera had predicted, Semele asked to see Zeus as he really was—no disguises. Zeus didn't want to, but he couldn't break his word. So, reluctantly, he revealed his true form. He shone like a bolt of lightning, and his radiance and power annihilated Semele. But though she died, her baby survived and grew up to be Hermes, the messenger god.

## HERA TAKES REVENGE ON IO

Io was a priestess of Hera, and by all accounts a very pretty woman. Unfortunately for her, Zeus agreed. When Hera found out about Zeus's attraction to Io, she confronted him, but he denied the whole thing and, just to be safe, turned Io into a cow to hide her. But then Hera asked for the pretty cow as a gift, and Zeus couldn't think of any plausible excuse for why she shouldn't have it. Hera tied the cow to a tree and kept it under the close watch of Argus, a giant whose hundred eyes made him very good at watching things.

Perhaps the most famous person Hera took revenge on was Heracles, who had the misfortune of being Zeus's son by another woman (see page 106).

But Zeus couldn't keep himself away. He got the messenger god Hermes to play his flute and put Argus to sleep and then kill him for good measure. Io was free! But she was still a cow.

Hera, of course, discovered what had happened. She commanded a gadfly to chase Io-cow and sting her over and over and over again. Io traveled for thousands of miles, trying and failing to get away from the stings, before Zeus finally changed her back into a person.

Moo
Mooo
Mooooooooo...

BITE!

TAKE IT FROM ME:
LOVE BITES!

# HERACLES

## THE HERO WHO BECAME A GOD

# HERACLES

**TRADITION:** Greek/Roman
**HOME:** Mount Olympus
**ALSO KNOWN AS:** Hercules (Roman)

Strong, nimble, and quick-witted, Heracles (pronounced "haira-kleez") is the most popular hero to come out of Greek mythology. Today he shows up in books, movies, TV shows, and video games, all telling, retelling, and sometimes even inventing myths about him. Unfortunately, this means that much of what people think they know about Heracles is at least partly wrong.

For one, he wasn't born a god. His father was the god Zeus, but his mother was just a human named Alcmene, and he spent his life on Earth. Hades, the god of the dead, never tried to kill him (they actually got along pretty well). Zeus's wife, Hera, *did* try to kill him, however. She was so angry that Zeus had cheated on her that she tried to prevent Heracles from being born. When that didn't work, she put snakes in his crib, but adorable baby Heracles squeezed them to death.

When Heracles grew up, he married a woman named Megara, and together they had five kids. But one night Hera used her magic to drive Heracles mad, and when he finally came to his senses, he found that he had killed his family. Alone and overwhelmed with grief, he sought the advice of the oracle at Delphi. The oracle told him to go serve King Eurystheus. If he completed the ten jobs the king gave him, Heracles wouldn't just be cleansed of his guilt—he would become immortal.

## THE ~~TEN~~ TWELVE LABORS OF HERACLES

The tasks King Eurystheus set for Heracles were clearly meant to kill him. For each one Heracles completed, the king grew more scared, barring Heracles from entering his city and from communicating through messengers. He also found reasons to claim some tasks didn't count, which is how Heracles' ten labors became twelve.

**1** **THE NEMEAN LION:** For his first task, Heracles killed a huge lion in the valley of Nemea. After showing the body to King Eurystheus, he skinned the lion using its own claws and made it into a cape, which he wore for the rest of his adventures.

**2** **THE LERNAEAN HYDRA:** Next, Heracles faced the Hydra, a huge, nine-headed, poisonous snake. What's worse, for every one of its heads that Heracles chopped off, two more grew back in its place. He might have died if it weren't for his buddy Iolaus, who stopped the head growth by burning the monster's neck stumps. They defeated the Hydra together, but since Heracles had help, King Eurystheus claimed the win didn't count.

**3** **THE CERYNEIAN HIND:** For his next task, Heracles had to capture the Ceryneian Hind, a golden-horned deer owned by the goddess Artemis. Heracles chased it for a year before he caught it, breaking one of its horns in the struggle. Artemis was angry, but she let Heracles off with a wärning.

**4** **THE ERYMANTHIAN BOAR:** Once again, Heracles had to capture an animal, and once again, he did. On the way, he ran into a tribe of centaurs who thought they could stop him from stealing their wine. They couldn't.

**5** **THE STABLES OF AUGEAS:** For Heracles' fifth labor, King Eurystheus loaned him to King Augeas, who owned the largest animal herds in all of Greece, as well as the most poop-filled stables. Augeas gave Heracles a day to clean his stables and promised him a tenth of his land if he managed it. Of course, he didn't expect Heracles to divert a river to do the cleaning for him, and King Augeas refused to give up his land. So Heracles fought a war against him, and then celebrated his victory with the first Olympic Games. Sadly, King Eurystheus decided the whole labor didn't count.

ALL THE POOP?

ALL THE POOP.

**6 THE STYMPHALIAN BIRDS:** These horrible birds lived on Lake Stymphalia. Heracles scared them into flight and shot them all with arrows.

**7 THE CRETAN BULL:** Next, Heracles captured a huge, violent bull in Crete and brought it back to King Eurystheus. It later escaped and rampaged all the way to Mount Olympus before being slain by another hero, Theseus.

**8 THE MARES OF DIOMEDES:** Diomedes was a barbarian chieftain whose horses ate human meat. Heracles raided Diomedes' camp and captured the horses. But his success came at a cost: They ate his friend Abduras. In revenge, he let them eat Diomedes, too.

**9 THE BELT OF HIPPOLYTA:** Hippolyta was the queen of the Amazons, a tribe of warrior women. Heracles asked for Hippolyta's belt, and she was happy to loan it to him. Unfortunately, Hera tricked the other Amazons into attacking, and Heracles killed them all.

**10 THE CATTLE OF GERYON:** Geryon, a three-bodied, four-winged giant, owned some beautiful red cows. Heracles sailed to Geryon's island in a big cup, killed the giant, and took the cattle.

**11 THE APPLES OF THE HESPERIDES:** Heracles' next task was to steal Zeus and Hera's golden apples, which were hidden in a secret garden and guarded by a dragon and a bunch of nymphs called the Hesperides. While searching for the apples, Heracles rescued Prometheus, who had been imprisoned by Zeus for giving fire to humans. As thanks, Prometheus directed Heracles to his brother, Atlas, who was stuck holding all the heavens on his shoulders. Atlas offered to go get the apples himself if Heracles held up the sky while he was gone. Heracles agreed. Atlas returned with the apples, but refused to take the sky back. Heracles asked Atlas to hold up the sky for just a few seconds while he got some padding for his shoulders. The moment Atlas took the sky, Heracles grabbed the apples and ran.

**12 THE HOUND CERBERUS:** Heracles' final task was to kidnap Cerberus, Hades' giant, three-headed dog. Heracles asked Hades if he could borrow Cerberus, and Hades said yes—but only if he could wrestle it into submission. Heracles did—then he took it to Eurystheus and returned it to Hades unharmed.

## HERACLES, THE GOD

His tasks completed, Heracles returned home and married a woman named Deianira. But their marriage was not a happy one, because Heracles fell in love with another woman, named Iole. Worried he might leave her forever, Deianira gave Heracles a cloak she had woven and secretly covered in a love potion she received from a centaur. As it turned out, the centaur had lied. The "potion" was a poison that caused unending pain. When she saw Heracles' agony, Deianira took her own life. Heracles, despairing and wracked with pain, prepared to burn himself to death.

> As a boy, Heracles was taught music by Apollo's son Linus . . . until Heracles got angry and killed Linus with a lute.

Finally, after Heracles had survived a lifetime of near deaths, impossible quests, and agonizing torture, Zeus intervened. He told Hera that Heracles had suffered enough, and Hera reluctantly agreed. They sent Athena to rescue him from the fire, cure his pain, and transform him into a god.

# HORUS

## PHARAOH OF THE GODS

## HORUS

**TRADITION:** Egyptian
**HOME:** The sky
**ALSO KNOWN AS:** Hor

In ancient Egyptian society, the pharaoh wasn't just a king. He (and occasionally she) was a living, breathing incarnation of the king of the gods, Horus. Horus is the ideal Egyptian king—a bold, just, and cunning leader who, while barely more than a boy, won his rightful kingdom back from the god who had usurped it. Since then, his reign has been peaceful and prosperous.

### HIDDEN BABY HORUS

Before Horus was born, his father, Osiris, was killed by his uncle, Seth. Osiris's body parts were scattered, and Seth took over the throne. As Osiris's son, Horus was the rightful pharaoh and a threat to Seth's power. His mother, Isis, kept him hidden for years, protecting him from all the supernatural baddies who wanted to finish what Seth had started.

PEEP PEEP

Once Horus was old enough, he left his mother's protection. He strode into Seth's royal court and, in front of all the assembled gods, declared himself the rightful pharaoh.

OBJECTION!!

What followed is one of the world's oldest recorded courtroom dramas. Seth and Horus both made their cases, and the assembled gods served as judge and jury. Horus had a strong argument—he was, after all, the rightful pharaoh by birth. Seth countered that, while Horus was Osiris's heir, he was also young, weak, and inexperienced. Egypt, he claimed, needed Seth's strength more than Horus's lineage. In the end, the gods ruled in favor of Horus, and Seth was removed from power—almost.

## The Eyes of Horus

The Eyes of Horus are one of the most common symbols in ancient Egyptian art and writing. Unlike the Eye of Ra, which is usually a poetic title for a goddess, the Eyes of Horus are usually Horus's actual eyes. There are lots of myths where someone (usually Seth) pokes, injures, hides, eats, and/or destroys one or both of Horus's eyes, and some other god helps restore them.

In some stories, the eyes represent the sun and the moon, which makes their destruction cataclysmic. That might be why rituals involving their renewal were performed in temples every month, timed with the cycles of the moon.

## HORUS'S DEATH-DEFYING SETH-DENYING

Seth had one plan left. He challenged Horus to a series of contests in order to prove that he would make the better pharaoh. They fought in the forms of ferocious animals and chased each other across the desert. More than once they injured each other. Seth tore out Horus's eyes, but Horus managed to get Seth pregnant, and Seth gave birth to the god of writing, Thoth. They even had a boat-making contest, which Horus won after Seth's boat sank (he made it out of rocks).

Eventually, Horus was declared the winner. Horus's dad, Osiris, who was now the king of the underworld, threatened to stop the world's crops from growing if Seth tried anything else. At long last, Horus became pharaoh.

In the end, even Seth ended up okay. As a consolation prize, he got to marry two of the sun god Ra's daughters and was given a great job as the guardian on the prow of Ra's solar boat, a position he has held ever since.

# INANNA

LADY OF HEAVEN

# INANNA

**TRADITION:** Sumerian/Mesopotamian

**HOME:** The heavens

**ALSO KNOWN AS:** Ishtar (Akkadian)

When you hear *love goddess*, you might expect someone kind, or caring, or at least sort of nice. Inanna's not that kind of love goddess. She can be sweet and convincing when she wants something, but at her core Inanna is about passion and power, seduction and slaughter. She's a goddess of love, yes, but also a goddess of war.

Inanna was one of the most important deities in ancient Mesopotamia. She is also one of the oldest goddesses on record, with evidence of her worship going back more than five thousand years. She seems to have started as a local fertility goddess in the city of Uruk. As that city gained importance, so did she, eventually being combined with another prominent (if slightly more violent) goddess named Ishtar.

As for her personality, legends vary. Some describe her as a coy young girl, others as a determined warrior, and still others as a conniving temptress, manipulating others to get what she wants. But don't mistake Inanna for evil. Her passion and fury can cause all sorts of problems, but sometimes it's just what's needed. As they say, all's fair in love and war.

## INANNA, ENKI, AND *ME*

Most of the greatest Mesopotamian gods had their own cities: Enki in Eridu, Enlil in Nippur, and Inanna in Uruk. Eridu was a great metropolis and home of the most advanced civilization, the first of its kind in all the world (or so the Sumerians believed). Uruk, on the other hand, was not so spectacular. So Inanna decided to visit Eridu and see if she could bring back knowledge.

URUK
(EEEEWW...)

ERIDU
(oooooooH!)

Inanna and her consort, Tammuz, are the subject of one of the oldest love poems in human history, but it's a little too risqué to repeat here.

When Inanna arrived at Eridu, Enki held a huge banquet in her honor. As one course led to the next, the day turned to night, and the two of them got very, very drunk. When Enki awoke the next morning, Inanna was gone, and so was Enki's *me* (pronounced *may*), a hundred tablets with all the foundational knowledge of civilization. Worse still, Enki's servants explained, it wasn't even a theft. Inanna had simply asked for the tablets, and Enki was so drunk that he said yes! Enki sent out monsters to retrieve the *me*.

There were seven stops on the route from Eridu to Uruk, and monsters attacked Inanna at each one. But monsters are no match for a goddess of love and war, and she made it back home unscathed. Once there, she read from the tablets and taught Uruk the secrets of civilization.

# INDRA

## THE KING OF STORMS

# INDRA

**TRADITION**: Indian/Hindu
**HOME**: Amaravati
**ALSO KNOWN AS**: Sakra

Summer in India means rain, and lots of it. Sometime in June, water starts pouring from the sky. In September, it stops. If you're a farmer, that's great, because you know when to plant and when to harvest. Nowadays we have some idea why it happens—hot air over land rises, drawing wet ocean air behind it, and the moisture then turns to rain. Ancient Indians had their own explanation: Indra.

Indra is the king of the gods in the Vedic religion of ancient India. He's a god of rain and storms, and a frighteningly strong warrior. His palace, floating in the clouds above Mount Meru, can vanish and reappear anywhere he chooses. He uses his bow, hook, and net to defend the gods and humanity from demons and natural disasters, all while riding a chariot that moves as fast as thought. He also drinks a lot of soma (like alcohol, but stronger), which, depending on the quantity, makes him either too strong to be beaten or too drunk to be conscious.

During the Vedic period (around 1500–500 BCE), Indra was the most important god in his pantheon. Holy books from that era dedicate more hymns to him than anyone else. But as the old Vedic religion gave way to modern Hinduism, his role diminished. He's still technically the king of the gods, but has been passed in importance by once minor gods like Vishnu and Shiva.

## THE GREAT CLOUD ROBBERY

Just like the people who worshipped them, the gods of ancient India kept herds of cattle. The difference was that while ancient Indians' cattle were hairy animals that made milk, Indra's cattle were puffy cloud cows that made rain. But herds of cattle—real or cloud—attract cattle thieves, and one day Indra awoke to find his cows had been stolen. No matter where he looked, he couldn't find them. So he sent out his servants, the Maruts, to continue the search and went to drink some soma.

Soon enough the Maruts returned. The cloud cows had been taken, they said, by the demon Vala, and hidden deep under a mountain where no one could reach them. But Vala hadn't counted on Indra's thunderbolts. One bolt and the mountain split open, releasing all the cloud cows back to the heavens.

## INDRA VS. VRITRA

Indra's most famous story describes his battle against Vala's bigger, meaner brother, Vritra. Vritra took the form of an enormous snake with ninety-nine coils and used his body to block the sources of all the world's water. Soon the lakes evaporated, the rivers ran dry, and the whole world fell into a drought. Without water, harvests failed and humanity began to starve. But though they heard the people begging for help, the gods were so afraid of Vritra that no one dared face him. No one, that is, except Indra.

Indra drank a bunch of soma and rode out to fight Vritra. Their battle was long and terrible, and the whole world shook as they traded blows. In the end, Indra hit Vritra with a thunderbolt, destroying him completely. With Vritra gone, the water flowed again and the world was saved.

### The Maruts

The Maruts are Indra's most loyal followers, brave warriors in golden armor who ride into battle at his side with thunderbolts raised. Some say they are sons of Rudra, the storm god who later evolved into Shiva. Others say they are sons of the goddess Diti. According to that story, Diti had planned to stay pregnant for a hundred years so she could give birth to a son as powerful as Indra. Indra, predictably, didn't want that. He forced her to give birth early, turning what might have been one powerful god into dozens of less powerful Maruts.

Another version of this story claims that while Indra fought Vritra, he couldn't defeat him, and Vishnu arranged a truce. Part of the agreement was that Indra couldn't attack Vritra with anything wet or dry, made of wood, metal, or stone, or at any time during the day or night. That barred every weapon known to ancient India and most weapons known to us now. But it didn't bar everything.

One evening as Indra walked by the sea, a huge column of foam burst out of the water. The foam wasn't wet or dry or made of wood, metal, or stone. And since it was the evening, it technically wasn't day or night. Indra grabbed the foam at once and smashed it into Vritra, killing him instantly. It turned out the foam was actually Vishnu, and this was all part of the plan.

The Indra vs. Vritra story also shows up in ancient Persian mythology, but in that version, Vritra is the good guy.

YOU'RE WELCOME!

# ISIS

THE GRIEVING GODDESS

## ISIS

**TRADITION:** Egyptian
**HOME:** The heavens
**ALSO KNOWN AS:** Aset, Eset

Love is surprisingly rare in Egyptian mythology. It's certainly a less common subject than birth, death, or kingship. But if you're looking for a truly loving figure, you can't go wrong with Isis.

Isis started out as a minor goddess, mostly just an extension of her husband, the god Osiris. But over time, as worship of Osiris and Isis spread, they gained new traits and absorbed other, lesser gods' myths and powers, eventually becoming two of the most worshipped gods in the Egyptian pantheon. Osiris became the lord of the underworld, while Isis became ancient Egypt's ideal woman, a caring daughter, loving wife, and loyal widow. And she didn't stop there. When Egypt was conquered by the Greeks and Romans, Isis's cult spread through those civilizations, too. She had major temples in Athens and Rome, and there's evidence that she had worshippers as far away as the British Isles.

## HOW ISIS WAS TEMPORARILY UNWIDOWED

Isis's husband, Osiris, was a great pharaoh. But his brother, Seth, coveted his throne and killed him to steal it. He cut Osiris's body up and hid it all over Egypt, and then declared himself pharaoh.

Osiris's death devastated Isis, but instead of just grieving, she decided to do something about it. She and her sister Nephthys traveled far and wide and gathered up all the bits of Osiris they could find. Once they had pieced him together, Isis used all her magic to bring him back . . . but it didn't work.

The only one who could bring someone back from the dead was the sun god, Ra, who died every night and was reborn every morning. Isis tricked Ra into loaning her some of his power, and then tried again to revive Osiris. This time it worked—sort of. It didn't work completely and it didn't work for long, but it worked long enough that Isis became pregnant with a son.

DO YOU HAVE HIS KNEE?

## THE RAISING OF THE PHARAOH

Isis knew from the moment she was pregnant that her baby would be powerful. She also knew that, as the son of the rightful pharaoh, he'd be in danger from the moment he was born. She hid baby Horus in a marsh and raised him in secret, teaching him, caring for him, and protecting him from beasts, monsters, and the usurper Seth.

When Horus came of age, he declared himself the rightful pharaoh in front of Seth and all the other gods. The stunned gods debated among themselves, but eventually came to a deadlock.

When Isis arrived to help her son, Seth kicked her out of the palace. But Isis was a clever and subtle goddess. She sneaked her way back in disguised as a young, beautiful follower of Seth. She asked for his help, saying that her son had been cheated out of his birthright—without revealing who her son really was. Seth agreed it was an outrage and promised that as soon as all this Horus nonsense was dealt with, he would help her son fix the injustice.

Then Isis removed her disguise and made sure all the gods knew what Seth had said: that her son had been unjustly cheated. At this, all the gods demanded that Horus be made pharaoh.

# IZANAMI
# AND IZANAGI

## THE GREAT ANCESTORS

## IZANAMI AND IZANAGI

**TRADITION:** Japanese/Shinto

**HOME:** Far Away and Yomi, respectively

**ALSO KNOWN AS:** Izanami-no-Mikoto (The August Female) and Izanagi-no-Mikoto (The August Male)

Izanami and Izanagi aren't the oldest Japanese gods, but they are the ones who formed the earth, created Japan, and more or less invented marriage and babies. They are sister and brother, wife and husband, and the parents of the most important gods and goddesses in the entire Shinto pantheon. But while they might have started out great, this isn't exactly a happily-ever-after kind of story.

## IZANAMI AND IZANAGI INVENT LAND

In the time of the first gods, Earth wasn't a planet. It was a vague, formless, watery thing. Izanami and Izanagi's first job as gods was to fix that. Standing on the edge of the bridge to heaven, they used a jeweled spear to stir it up. Then they pulled the spear out and held it steady, letting the goop it had collected drip back down. Wherever the drips landed, they created land, starting with the island of Onogoro. Their work done, Izanami and Izanami went to Onogoro, erected a ceremonial pillar, and decided to have babies.

SPLOOSH!!!

## IZANAMI AND IZANAGI INVENT MARRIAGE AND BABIES

No one had ever made babies before, and Izanami and Izanagi weren't sure how to do it. They walked around their island pillar in opposite directions, thus performing the world's first marriage ceremony. Then they shouted with joy and embraced. In due course Izanami gave birth to the islands that make up Japan and then to a bunch of gods and goddesses. But the couple's happiness didn't last.

Giving birth to the fire god, Kagutsuchi, left Izanami so badly burned that she died. Even in death, more gods emerged. They came from her poop, pee, and vomit, from Izanagi's tears, and from Kagutsuchi's blood after Izanagi, in a grief-stricken rage, cut off his head.

## IZANAMI AND IZANAGI INVENT DIVORCE

Once Izanagi recovered enough to think, he decided that, one way or another, he would get Izanami back. He journeyed across the world and into the underworld, searching its depths for his love. At long last he found her, deep in a cave, shrouded in shadows. But when he asked her to return with him, she told him she couldn't. She had eaten the food of the underworld, and it had bound her there. She said she would plead with the underworld gods to be released, but made Izanagi promise not to try to see her until she was allowed to go free.

Izanagi agreed to wait, but he longed to see her. Eventually, he gave in to temptation, lit a torch, and approached his wife. But as the light illuminated her, Izanagi stopped, horrified. This wasn't the Izanami he remembered. In death, she had become a rotting, maggoty corpse. He turned and fled.

...IS THERE SOMETHING IN MY TEETH?

Izanami, hurt and outraged that Izanagi had broken his promise, sent hags, monsters, and gods after him, but he held them off with speed, luck, and some magical peaches. As he raced to the exit of the underworld, Izanami herself came for him, but he blocked her path with a boulder and escaped to the surface. Izanami shouted a final threat: If he divorced her, she would kill mortals every day. He countered that he would give life to even more. Ever since then, people have died, but even more have been born.

# THE JADE EMPEROR

## HEAD OF THE CELESTIAL BUREAUCRACY

# THE JADE EMPEROR

**TRADITION:** Chinese/Taoist/Buddhist
**HOME:** The Celestial Palace Heavenly Court
**ALSO KNOWN AS:** Yuhuang Shangdi (Jade August
Supreme Lord), Tian (Heaven), Yu Di (Jade Emperor)

The Jade Emperor, Yuhuang Shangdi, is the current head of a pantheon that's a mixture of Taoist, Buddhist, Confucian, and older Chinese mythology. He is an idealized version of a Chinese emperor: wise, virtuous, brave, and just. The Jade Emperor was officially declared head of the Celestial Bureaucracy by the emperor of China in 1007 CE.

## THE GREAT BUREAUCRACY IN THE SKY

The Chinese pantheon of gods and goddesses is organized a lot like the medieval Chinese state. At the top is the emperor, surrounded by his family and a bunch of nobles, clerks, servants, and assistants, each of whom oversees their own nobles, clerks, servants and assistants, and so on. The Jade Emperor's chief assistant alone is in charge of seventy-five fully staffed departments.

And it's not just gods—as different ideas and religions have entered China, the Celestial Bureaucracy has grown to include them. Gods and goddesses, dead emperors and empresses, Buddhas, bodhisattvas, enlightened immortals, and a variety of other supernatural folks attend to an ever-expanding list of departments and duties, planning, organizing, and recording everything that happens in our world. And as the world changes, so does the bureaucracy—Buddhist ideas of karma and reincarnation, for instance, led to whole new departments that track how folks live their lives and what reincarnations they deserve.

For the most part, people didn't pray directly to the Jade Emperor. That would be like knocking on the door of the White House and asking to meet with the president. Instead, they would go through one of the thousands of ministers and judges and bureaucrats who made up the Celestial Bureaucracy.

## HOW THE JADE EMPEROR BECAME THE JADE EMPEROR

Long before he was an emperor, Yu Di was a human prince. His parents, the king and queen, had struggled for ages to conceive a son, and they asked their priests to pray on their behalf.

The next night, the queen dreamed that the god Laozi approached her, carrying a baby boy in his arms. The next morning she woke up to find herself pregnant.

Their son grew up to be brilliant, kind, and humble. When he inherited the kingdom, he gave it up, choosing instead to lead a simple life of work and contemplation. He spent his time healing the sick and helping the poor, and when he died, he became the assistant to the Celestial Emperor Yuanshi Tianzun, the Primeval Lord of Heaven. When Yuanshi Tianzun chose to retire, he could think of no one more deserving than Yu Di to succeed him.

## The Officials of the Celestial Bureaucracy

The Celestial Bureaucracy is made up of a variety of folks from a variety of religions and mythologies, including Taoism, Buddhism, and Chinese folk religions, among others. Here are just a few types you might run into:

**Gods/goddesses:** Deities from Chinese folk religion—some local, some widely revered, some dating back thousands of years.

**Buddhas:** People who achieved nirvana, a state of enlightened transcendence in which one is free of all suffering and desire and is released from the cycle of death and rebirth.

**Bodhisattvas:** People who achieved nirvana, but chose to postpone their exit from our world in order to help others do the same.

**Immortals:** The greatest Taoist practitioners who achieved immortality, including Laozi, founder of Taoism, and the Eight Immortals, a group of arguably historical people who have become legends.

**Dead emperors/empresses:** Some historical Chinese rulers went on to serve in the Celestial Bureaucracy after their deaths.

A variety of other supernatural folks have also been appointed to the bureaucracy over the years. The most famous of them is probably Sun Wukong, the Monkey King (see page 226).

## How We Know What We Know About Chinese Mythology

Chinese mythology can get pretty confusing, especially if you are new to it. It's a combination of so many different religions, philosophies, and belief systems that it can be hard to know where to begin. Here are just a few of the major sources of Chinese mythology:

- **Ancient Chinese art and texts:** Most knowledge of the religion of the earliest Chinese civilizations has been lost to time, but some writing and art have survived. From these, we get a picture of a religion with a wide variety of gods and goddesses, although many of them remain mysterious.

- **Confucian writings:** Confucianism is one of the most influential Chinese philosophies, and while its creator, Confucius, didn't have much to say about gods or myths, his later followers built up a mythology around his birth, life, and death that connected him with other mythical creatures and characters.

- **Taoist writings:** Taoism, which arose around the same time as Confucianism, incorporated a whole pantheon of gods, heroes, and spirits. Later, Taoists integrated Confucius, ancient Chinese gods, and various folk myths into the Celestial Bureaucracy.

- **Buddhist writings:** A few hundred years after that, Buddhism arrived in China, adding even more deities and stories and concepts and making big changes to Chinese views of the afterlife.

← | →

- MINISTRY OF INCARNATION
- MINISTRY OF REINCARNATION
- MINISTRY OF PREINCARNATION
- MINISTRY OF SPIRITS
- MINISTRY OF GHOSTS
- MINISTRY OF DEMONS

- MINISTRY OF WAR
- MINISTRY OF PEACE
- MINISTRY OF TRADE
- MINISTRY OF FARMING
- MINISTRY OF WEATHER
- MINISTRY OF MINISTRIES

# KALI

## THE DARK GODDESS

## KALI

**TRADITION:** Hindu/Indian
**ALSO KNOWN AS:** Kalika

All the greatest Hindu goddesses are incarnations of the great goddess Devi (which means, literally, "goddess"). Most of them are reflections of her most popular qualities: her wisdom, her kindness, her discipline, her love. But when you're eye to ankle with a mile-high demon, you don't want kindness. You want someone powerful enough to send that demon back where it came from, in pieces if necessary. You want someone like Kali.

She certainly cuts a striking image, with her black hair, red tongue, necklace of heads, and skirt of arms. But Kali is more complicated than her grisly look might suggest. Her name is the female form of the old Sanskrit word *kala*, which means "time," and that's closer to what she represents. Kali, like time, is powerful, endless, and (with one or two exceptions) unstoppable.

## THE BIRTH(S) OF KALI

There are many conflicting accounts of Kali's birth. Here are a few of the more popular stories:

### The Parvati-Poison Birth

Once, a demon named Daruka attacked the gods, and they were helpless to stop him. He could only be killed by a woman, and the only gods who could fight (in this story, at least) were men. In desperation, they went to Shiva's wife, Parvati, for help. Now, Parvati was no warrior, but she agreed to do what she could and dove headfirst into Shiva's throat.

A long time before any of this, Shiva had swallowed a horrible poison. He only survived the experience because Parvati had stopped it before it reached his stomach. But some remained in his throat and turned it a permanent, unhealthy blue.

When Parvati entered Shiva's throat, she merged with that poison. When she came back out, she had transformed into Kali. Daruka never had a chance.

## The Combined Powers Birth

The gods once came under attack by another demon named Raktabija. Raktabija wasn't invincible—the gods could hurt him just fine—but that was the problem. Wherever his blood hit the ground, it created fresh new demon soldiers to fight for him.

With every wound, Raktabija's army grew, until the gods were besieged on all sides. As a last resort, the gods came together and combined their energy, using it to create the one thing that could defeat Raktabija: Kali.

Kali handled the demons like a divine vacuum cleaner, swallowing them whole. Once she ate her way to Raktabija, she grabbed him by the hair, chopped off his head, and drank every last drop of his blood before any could touch the ground.

## The Angry-Durga Birth

Durga is another Hindu warrior goddess. She's always had a temper, particularly where demons are concerned. Once, while fighting an especially awful demon, she got so furious that her anger itself became a new goddess, Kali, who burst from her forehead ready to kill. Kali went on a rampage, killing, eating, and destroying everything in her path.

At first the gods were elated—look at all the demons she slayed! But as time went on, and she didn't stop, they realized they might have a problem. It was Shiva who finally managed to stop her. As Kali continued her killing rampage, he quietly lay down in her path and waited. A few seconds later, the shock of realizing she had just stomped on the Destroyer himself calmed Kali down.

# K I N T U

## THE FIRST MAN

# KINTU

**TRADITION:** East African
**HOME:** Buganda (part of modern Uganda)

Uganda, in the eastern part of Africa, is home to a huge number of peoples, cultures, languages, and myths. Most of these myths are local, and few people outside of those regions know anything about them. But a few have spread widely enough that they show up all over the place. One is the story of the clever hero Kintu and his trip to heaven for a wife.

## KINTU'S TRIP TO HEAVEN FOR A WIFE

Long ago, before the world was full of people, Kintu was alone and lonely. All he had for company was a cow, and all he had for food was its milk. One day a girl named Nambi, who lived in the heavens, looked down and saw Kintu. She fell instantly, deeply in love with him, but her family didn't approve. They thought Kintu looked wimpy, sitting alone and drinking milk. And to prove what a wimp he was, they sneaked down and stole his cow. Now Kintu was even more alone, and out of milk to boot.

The first chance she got, Nambi came down, told Kintu where his cow was, and brought him back up with her to retrieve it. When they got to Nambi's home, her father, Gulu, welcomed them both with a feast large enough to feed half a tribe—and told Kintu to eat it all, or he would kill him. Then Gulu left, laughing to himself and taking Nambi with him.

Kintu ate and ate and ate until he was nearly bursting, but he barely made a dent in the pile. He searched the room for anything that might help. Discovering a hole under the floor, he shoveled the rest of the food into it. When Gulu returned, he was stunned to find Kintu surrounded by empty plates.

Next, Gulu handed Kintu a copper ax and told him to go cut firewood—from a rock. Kintu got lucky and found a rock that was already full of cracks. By pulling at it with all his strength, he managed to break off some stone chunks. Imagine Gulu's surprise when Kintu returned, ax intact, and handed him the "firewood."

Then Gulu gave Kintu a huge pot and told him to fill it with water—but he wouldn't accept water from any river, lake, pond, or well. Kintu brought the pot outside and searched for a different kind of water, but without success. Eventually he fell asleep. When he woke up, he found he had lucked out again: The pot was full of morning dew.

Kintu had now completed three impossible tasks. Gulu congratulated Kintu and said he would give him his cow back and even allow him to marry Nambi. But first, Kintu had to work out which one of Gulu's thousands of cows was his.

This time Kintu couldn't do it alone, so he found a bee who agreed to help him by hovering over the correct cow. The next morning, when Kintu and Gulu went out to the herds, the bee waited by a tree. Kintu told Gulu that his cow wasn't there. Then they went to another herd, and the bee buzzed around another tree, and Kintu told Gulu that his cow wasn't there, either. When they got to the third herd, the bee flew around a cow and then around three newborn calves. Kintu pointed to all of them and told them that they were all his cows—the cow that Gulu had stolen, and that cow's babies.

Gulu was amazed and finally gave in. Kintu and Nambi could marry. But when they left the heavens for Kintu's home on Earth, Gulu gave them a warning: They had to go quickly and not come back, or else Nambi's brother, Walumbe (*Death*), would follow them.

They did as Gulu said until Nambi realized she had forgotten the food for her pet chick. Kintu tried to stop her, but she ran back to get it, and when she returned, Walumbe was with her. When Kintu and Nambi settled on Earth, Walumbe moved in as well, and death has been killing people ever since.

# LEIZU

## THE GODDESS OF SILK

# LEIZU

**TRADITION:** Chinese
**HOME:** The Heavenly Court
**ALSO KNOWN AS:** Lady Silkworm, Can Nü

One of China's most unique goddesses is tied to one of China's most unique and treasured materials: silk.

There are a few competing stories about where Leizu, or Lady Silkworm, came from and who she is. In one story, she is a goddess of the night sky. In another, she's the wife of the mythical Yellow Emperor, Huang Di.

## THE EMPEROR'S WIFE

According to this story, Leizu is the wife of the Yellow Emperor, a legendary Chinese deity. One afternoon, she discovered some cocoons in a mulberry tree. Curious, she took some with her as she went for her afternoon tea. When she went to drink, she accidentally dropped one into her cup. The hot water made the cocoon unravel, and she pulled and pulled at the string until she had unwound it all from the worm inside.

*WHAT IN THE...?*

She then convinced her husband, the emperor, to give her some mulberry trees to experiment with. She learned to domesticate the worms and invented many of the tools the ancient Chinese used to make silk thread and fabric.

## THE LEGEND OF LADY SILKWORM

In a less common but more fanciful story, the goddess of silk started as a farmer's daughter. She was a beautiful, kind, and loyal girl, and when her father had to leave on business, she took perfect care of their home until he returned.

People have been making silk cloth since at least the 2000s BCE. It's comfortable, light, strong, and beautiful, and it was in demand all across the ancient world—which is why the world's most famous trade route, running from China through Asia and into the Middle East, was called the Silk Road. The process of silk manufacturing—the cultivation of silkworms and the harvesting of fiber from their cocoons—was a carefully kept secret even within China itself. No one outside of Asia managed to make silk cloth until the 500s CE, when the Byzantine Emperor Justinian had some Persian monks sneak silkworms and mulberry seeds out of China, stored in hollow chambers in their canes.

YOU DIDN'T GET THIS FROM ME.

But one of his trips went longer than expected, and as days turned into weeks and months, she began to worry. After more than a year, she had nearly lost hope. She remarked while brushing the family's horse that she would willingly marry anyone who could bring her father home. At that, the horse reared and galloped away. The girl gave chase, but it was too fast. Soon it was over the horizon, and she had no choice but to return home, now missing a father and a horse.

A few days later the stallion found her father. He was completely unconcerned about having left his daughter for so long, but when he recognized his own horse, stamping and whinnying and shaking its head, he feared the worst. Was his daughter in trouble? He leaped on and rode off.

When they returned home, the daughter was overjoyed. The father, too, appreciated the horse's actions and gave it extra food from then on. The horse seemed to appreciate the gesture, but as the days passed, the father noticed that it wasn't always happy. The horse got very upset whenever it saw his daughter. When the farmer asked his daughter if she knew why, she admitted that she promised to marry anyone who brought her father home. Her father was aghast and ordered her to keep it secret. He killed the horse, skinned it, and hung its hide to dry, preparing to make it into leather.

It wasn't long before her father had to leave again, promising to return soon. Later that day, his daughter walked along with a friend, talking and laughing and enjoying themselves. As they passed the horse's hide, it began to move. It rose up behind the girl, floating like a ghost, and then swooped over her, wrapping her up and dragging her away. Her friend couldn't catch her, and soon the girl was out of sight.

When the farmer got home, his daughter's sobbing friend told him what had happened. It took him days to find her, still wrapped in horsehide, dangling from a mulberry tree. But she wasn't the daughter he remembered. She had turned into the world's first silkworm. When she opened her mouth, a fine, beautiful thread came out: the world's first silk.

NEEEEIIGGHHH…..

# LOKI

## THE DECEITFUL JERK

# LOKI

**TRADITION:** Norse
**HOME:** Asgard, then Hel

If you remember one thing about Loki, remember this: Loki is a jerk. Sometimes he's a jerk to the gods' enemies, and sometimes to the gods themselves. Sometimes he's just annoying, like when he crashed the gods' dinner party just to insult everyone there. But sometimes he is truly destructive, like when he planned the death of poor Baldr. At Ragnarok, the great battle at the end of the world, it's Loki's boat that will bring the giants to fight the gods, and Loki who will kill the gods' watchman, Heimdall.

But Loki isn't totally evil, or at least not all the time. There's evidence that people emphasized his worst qualities as Christianity spread through Scandinavia— which happens to be when most of what we know about him was written down. It didn't help that he had some things in common with the Christian devil.

Although he appears in lots of Norse legends, Loki wasn't ever worshipped by many people. It makes sense if you think about it—he only does what anyone wants when they threaten to kill him. Best to leave a god like that alone.

## THE KIDNAPPING (AND UNKIDNAPPING) OF IDUN

One day while traveling, Loki and the gods Odin and Hoenir got hungry. They killed an ox and tried to cook it, but no matter how long they held its meat in the fire, it wouldn't heat up. A little while later, an eagle landed nearby and said that the meat wasn't cooking because the eagle had enchanted it. But if the gods promised to let the eagle eat its fill, it would allow the meat to cook. The gods reluctantly agreed.

But the eagle ate all the tastiest parts, so Loki hit it with a branch—or tried to. As he swung it, the eagle grabbed hold and took flight. Loki was dragged up and up and up into the sky. Then the eagle revealed itself to be a giant named Thjazi and refused to bring Loki back down until he promised to help Thjazi kidnap the goddess Idun and her fruits of immortality. Loki agreed.

Loki found Idun and tricked her into bringing her fruit outside the walls of Asgard. As soon as she was unprotected, Thjazi burst out and kidnapped her.

Without Idun and her youth-restoring fruits, the gods of Asgard grew gray and wrinkled. Eventually, they realized that the last time anyone had seen Idun, she had been leaving Asgard with Loki.

The gods grabbed Loki and forced him to tell them what he did. Then they made it clear that if he didn't get Idun back they would punish him.

Loki turned into a hawk and flew to Thjazi's home. As luck would have it, Thjazi was out on a fishing trip, so Loki turned Idun into a nut, picked her up in his beak, and carried her away as fast as his wings could fly. But when Thjazi returned, he saw what had happened and flew after them. When the gods in Asgard saw them coming, they prepared a big pile of wood and tinder. As soon as Loki passed overhead, they lit it on fire. Thjazi had no time to change course before he flew into the flames.

WHERE'S LOKI?

WHO'S SOAKY?

## Yggdrasil, the World Tree

The world, in Norse mythology, is a huge, impossibly tall ash tree called Yggdrasil. Several cosmic animals live in the tree, acting for good or ill. Four deer chew on its branches, although two of them also help restore the tree with mead and water. In the highest branches lives a great eagle. And down below, the dragon Nidhogg gnaws on the tree's roots, slowly destabilizing the universe.

In its branches and roots, Yggdrasil holds nine separate worlds, including Asgard (the home of the Aesir gods), Vanaheim (the home of the Vanir gods), Hel (the underworld), and Midgard (the middle world where we live). The other worlds are home to giants, elves, and dark elves (also known as dwarfs).

## HOW LOKI BECAME A MOTHER

One day, a giant arrived at Asgard to offer his services. He said he could build the gods a wall so thick and strong that it would withstand any attack. What's more, he could complete it in only three seasons. Then he named his price: He would get the sun and the moon, and he would marry the love goddess Freya.

The gods convened to discuss the offer. Freya was against it, of course, but Loki thought it was a good idea. He suggested they accept, but give the giant impossible conditions: He had to complete the wall in only one winter, and no one except the giant's horse could help him. To everyone's surprise, the giant accepted.

Eventually, the gods got sick of Loki's antics and imprisoned him. Now he's bound at the base of the world tree, with snakes dripping venom in his eyes.

He worked fast, and his horse worked faster, hauling huge stones across the land at impossible speeds. With three days left in winter, and the wall nearly finished, the gods began to panic. They summoned Loki and told him to fix the problem or they would kill him.

That night, Loki turned himself into a lady horse and caught the stallion's attention. Then he raced away, the stallion following in hot pursuit. When the giant saw that his stallion was gone, he and the gods both knew he couldn't complete the wall in time. Thor killed the giant with his hammer.

A while later, Loki (still in horse form) gave birth to a magical, eight-legged horse named Sleipnir, who became Odin's trusted steed.

MAMA!

NO.

# MAUI

## THE HERO OF THE PACIFIC

# MAUI

**TRADITION:** Maori/Polynesian
**HOME:** Various islands in the Pacific

**O**f all the mythological characters from the islands of the Pacific, none is as well known as Maui. Most sources agree that Maui was human, but he went toe-to-toe with all sorts of gods and supernatural beings. He was a rebel, a trickster, and a seducer who ignored laws and taboos and changed the way the world works and the role of people in it. Below are just a few of the many stories about Maui told by the indigenous groups in the Pacific.

## MAUI'S GRANDMOTHER'S JAWBONE

When Maui was a boy, his mother spent all day weaving fibers into cloth, but no matter how hard she tried, she could never finish her work before the sun set and it got too dark to see. Maui promised himself that, one way or another, he would solve her problem.

Maui's chance came when his grandmother died and he came into possession of her enchanted jawbone. The next morning he followed the sun up into the sky and used the jawbone to beat the living daylights out of it. He beat it so badly that from then on, the sun could only crawl across the sky, and the days became long enough for his mother to finish her work.

Later, Maui brought the jawbone on a fishing trip with his brothers. They sailed out, dropped their fishing lines, and waited for something to bite. Suddenly, Maui's line went taut. He had hooked something huge—so huge that he couldn't reel it in even with the help of his brothers.

The Hawaiian island of Maui is not named after this particular Maui—but it might be named after someone who was named after this Maui.

They tried a second time, but the line snapped before they could see what they had caught. The third time, they finally managed to reel it in, but the "fish" turned out to be nothing of the sort. It was a whole island! Specifically, it was New Zealand's northern island. Maui's fishing hook, which in some versions of the story is his grandmother's old jawbone, became crescent-shaped Hawke Bay.

## MAUI'S DEATH-DEFYING DEATH

Sources differ on how Maui died—in an accident or a fight, in the ocean or in the sky—but perhaps the most interesting story comes from New Zealand.

Maui, they say, died in the pursuit of immortality. He heard that the underworld goddess Hine-nui-te-po held the secret source of life inside her body, and he figured if he stole it, he would live forever. He went to the underworld with several of his brothers, all disguised as birds. When they found the sleeping Hine-nui-te-po, he warned his bird-brothers not to laugh or make any noise, lest they wake her up. Then Maui stripped naked and started crawling inside Hine-nui-te-po to begin his search. One of his bird-brothers couldn't help but laugh. Hine-nui-te-po woke up with Maui still inside her and, as punishment, crushed him to death. Ever since, no human has been immortal.

SHHH

# MITHRA

## THE GOD WHO GOT AROUND

# MITHRA

**TRADITION:** Persian/Indian/Roman
**HOME:** Various (usually the sky)
**ALSO KNOWN AS:** Mitra (Indian), Mithras (Roman)

Not many gods have lasted as long or traveled as far as Mithra. There is evidence of his worship from prehistory to 300 CE, in areas stretching from India to England. Even more interesting, it wasn't all continuous. He would lose importance in one civilization and seem to disappear, only to find new worshippers, hundreds of years later and thousands of miles away.

Despite the wide range in time and place, all versions of Mithra have a few things in common. He's a god of light and sunshine, a guardian of friendships, contracts, and oaths. He defends the order of the universe—sky above, Earth below, people in the middle, and everything working as it should.

## MITRA IN INDIA

The first versions of Mithra on record come from India and Persia. In India, he was called Mitra and had a twin brother named Varuna—together, they were gods of light, order, and agreements. Mitra was the friendlier of the two and handled alliances between humans, while Varuna dealt with the relationships between humans and gods. They judged mortal actions, and people prayed to them for forgiveness, protection, or help avoiding the consequences of the bad things they had done.

There's some evidence that Mitra might have been more important in prehistory, but by the time folks started writing stuff down (around 1000 BCE), he wasn't one of the top gods. As the ancient Vedic religion gave way to modern Hinduism, Mitra worship continued to decline, and while he is still a part of the Hindu pantheon, he isn't mentioned much.

## MITHRA IN PERSIA

At the same time as Mitra was fading in India, he was gaining worshippers in Persia as Mithra, and by 500 BCE, he was the most important god in the Persian pantheon. The Persians seem to have created a bull-sacrificing ceremony that stuck with Mithra for centuries. It's possible that this was related to an Indian story where Mitra sacrificed a god named Soma, who sometimes appeared as a white bull.

In Persia, Mithra's role as a god of order encouraged loyalty to the king, which might have been part of its success—loyalty makes kings happy, so state religions tend to encourage it.

When the Persian Empire converted to a new religion, Zoroastrianism, most of the old Persian pantheon fell away. But Mithra held on, mostly in the western reaches of the empire but also in the capital itself. But then, around 330 BCE, a Greek guy named Alexander the Great conquered Persia, and Mithra (along with a lot of ancient Persian culture) largely disappeared.

WE WORSHIP MITHRA NOW!

## MITHRAS IN ROME

For hundreds of years after Alexander, Mithra was hardly mentioned. He still had worshippers, but they were pretty rare and mostly in one small area of the eastern Mediterranean. In the meantime, Greece was conquered by Rome, which was near the apex of its power by the time Mithra showed up again, now called Mithras.

Suddenly, in 136 CE, Mithras was everywhere. There were hundreds of inscriptions dedicating stuff to him, and worship seems to have spread through the military, the government, and society at large. There's evidence of Mithras worship across the Roman world, as far away as modern-day France and England. The strange part is, no one is really sure why. Was it a political thing? Was there some super influential Mithras prophet that we have lost all record of? No one knows.

## The Mystery Religions

We know a lot about Greek and Roman religions. Their pantheons are probably the best known in the world, and their gods are the first thing a lot of folks think of when they hear the word *mythology*. But the ancient Romans and Greeks also had mystery religions.

These were the secret clubs of the religious world, with secret meetings, secret teachings, and secret ceremonies. If you weren't a member of the club, you weren't allowed to know much about it. Some were focused on secret gods, but more were focused on secret knowledge of well-known gods such as Demeter or Dionysus.

Roman Mithraism was a very different religion from its Persian ancestor. It was what scholars call a mystery religion—a secret religion, separate from the imperial cult, known only to its initiates. It also had a strict no-girls-allowed policy. Mithras himself was still a god of the sun and promises, but now with a heavy emphasis on the relationship between kings and their soldiers.

Mithras worship ended at the same time as most other parts of Roman paganism and for the same reason: Christianity. A bunch of Romans converted to Christianity, and then an Emperor did, and then most of the rest of them did, and that was that. Goodbye, Mithras.

SECRET CHURCH OF MITHRA

PASSWORD?

# MONSTERS

## (AND OTHER FEROCIOUS BEASTS)

We have always been wary of the unknown. It's a big part of why we have mythology—to answer questions to which there are (or were) no easy answers. Why are we here? Where did we come from? How should we live? What's out there, in the wilderness, beyond the edge of civilization? And why is it drooling?

Here are a few of the most famous mythological monsters.

## AQRABUAMELU

Sumerian myths tell of enormous creatures that are human from the waist up but have a scorpion's legs and poisonous tail. They are vicious warriors at close range and deadly accurate with their bows and arrows. Thankfully, the scorpion-men are protectors, not raiders. With a few exceptions (like helping the hero Gilgamesh) they stay in place, guarding the palace of the sun god Shamash and other important sites.

## BEDAWANG

Bedawang, the cosmic turtle of Balinese mythology, emerged from the world-serpent Antaboga's meditation. He holds the entire world on his back, along with a writhing pile of snakes and an enormous black rock that marks the entrance to the underworld. When you're as big as Bedawang, everything you do has major effects—when he stirs, it causes earthquakes and volcanic eruptions.

## ECHIDNE

Echidne (sometimes written as Echidna) is one of the oldest Greek monsters, a half-woman, half-snake daughter of the earth goddess Gaia. Her marriage to the fire-breathing giant Typhon produced some of the most fearsome creatures in Greek mythology, including Hades' dog Cerberus, the hundred-headed dragon Orthus, the sea monster Scylla, and the Nemean lion that nearly killed Heracles.

## FENRIR

The average wolf has nothing on Fenrir, the great, ravenous beast of Norse mythology. He's the son of Loki and a giant named Angrboda. At first the gods thought they could tame him, or at least keep him under control. But as he grew bigger and stronger, they decided to trap him with an impossibly strong dwarf-forged chain, costing the god Tyr his hand in the process. But even the strongest chain in the world can't hold Fenrir forever. When Ragnarok, the end of the world, arrives, he's destined to break free and devour the king of the gods, Odin, as well as everything else in his path.

YOU MIGHT SAY I'LL WOLF HIM DOWN.

## MANTICORE

In ancient Persia, rumors spread of a monster from the east, a red lion with a humanlike head and three rows of sharpened teeth. At the end of its tail were long, poisonous quills, which it shot like darts at its prey. Anyone hit by them died instantly and was gobbled up so completely that not even a bone was left behind.

## MINOTAUR

The Greek sea god, Poseidon, once punished the king of Crete by making his queen fall in love with a bull, resulting in an enormous son with the head and tail of a bull—the Minotaur. The king locked the Minotaur in the world's largest maze, called the labyrinth. Every year, he sent seven boys and seven girls from the rival kingdom of Athens into the labyrinth as food for the Minotaur. Years later, the hero Theseus defeated the beast, with the help of the king's daughter Ariadne. She sneaked Theseus some thread, which he tied at the entrance of the maze and slowly unraveled as he searched inside. When he found the Minotaur, he beat it to death, and then followed the thread back out.

## ONI

Japanese legends tell of cruel demons called oni. They are shaped like humans, but bigger and beefier, with brightly colored skin, horns, and three eyes. Some hunt with their sharp claws, while others wield huge spiked clubs. Stories claim that they fly around stealing the souls of evil people. Once a year, the traditional oni-yarabi ceremony is held to drive them away.

## RAKSHASA

Rakshasas are evil spirits in ancient Hindu myth. They come in a wide variety of shapes and sizes, with bizarre numbers of heads and limbs, and are almost always ugly. Cruel, cunning creatures, they spend their time eating people, ruining rituals, and desecrating graves. Their former king, Ravana, was defeated by Rama, an incarnation of the Hindu god Vishnu.

I. UM. ER. DOUBLE OR NOTHING?

## SPHINX

The sphinx has a somewhat complicated history. In ancient Egypt, it was usually a symbol of kings, while in ancient Assyrian myths, it served as a temple guardian. In Greek myth, the sphinx was a cunning monster, a lion with an eagle's wings and a beautiful woman's head. It sat on a rock near the road to Thebes and demanded that travelers answer its riddle: What animal has four feet in the morning, two at noon, and three in the evening? When they failed to answer, the sphinx jumped down and killed them. Finally, a man named Oedipus answered it correctly: a person, who crawls on all fours as a baby, walks on two feet as an adult, and then hobbles with a staff (the third "foot") as an old person. Upon hearing the correct answer, the sphinx killed itself.

## THUNDERBIRD

The thunderbird is common to myths all across North America. It's a colossal bird, with eyes that create lightning and wings so huge that their beating causes thunder. Some say it's a spirit or even a god. Others say it's an actual animal that nests on mountaintops. Most accounts say the bird is well meaning but dangerously powerful. Next time there's a storm, listen closely, and you might just hear its cry in the thunder.

## WENDIGO

Native legends of the American Northeast say the winter fog hides a horrible beast. It's shaped like a person, but huge and foul smelling, with a mouth full of jagged teeth and a taste for people. In some tellings, wendigos used to be human but were transformed by eating human flesh.

# THE MORRÍGNA

## THE SISTERS OF WAR

# THE MORRÍGNA

**TRADITION:** Celtic
**HOME:** The battlefield

The ancient Celtic religion was full of goddesses, often associated with specific villages, rivers, forests, or hills. These were mostly local goddesses, unknown beyond their immediate surroundings. Nowadays, we hardly know about any of them—an inscription here, an allusion there, but not enough to say anything certain about their myths. But there are exceptions, including the three sisters of the Morrígna.

Celtic mythology is full of threes—triple births, triple deaths, and especially triple gods and goddesses. The Morrígna are one such trio, powerful goddesses who use their dark magic to create and influence war, chaos, terror, and death. Their descriptions, traits, and stories can be hard to tell apart, and there's even some evidence that they might be the same goddess, but they are listed separately here as the Morrígan, the Badb, and Nemain.

## THE MORRÍGAN

*Morrígan* means "Queen of Phantoms," and the Morrígan lives up to her name. She haunts battlefields and scoops up doomed soldiers, washing the blood from them as they die.

She doesn't wield any weapons—instead, she uses her magic to sap soldiers' strength, turning battles against them. On those rare occasions when she does fight directly, it's always in the shape of an animal. In one famous battle, she became an eel and tripped up the hero Cú Chulainn as he fought in a river, then she turned into a wolf that sent panicked cattle stampeding against him, and then she became the white-and-red cow that led the stampede. Cú Chulainn managed to injure her and win the battle, but she had her revenge. Later, when Cú Chulainn finally lost a battle, she turned into a crow and perched on his shoulder as he died.

BATH TIME...

No! No BATH! No BATH!!

## THE BADB

If you ever see the Badb, you are probably doomed. She's an omen of death—she won't kill you, but something will. She usually takes the form of a crow or hag, hanging around the battlefield, but has been known to take other forms, too.

Once, Cú Chulainn was woken by a scream so terrible that even he was scared.

The plural form of the word *Badb*, *badba*, is also the collective name for some other supernatural beings who haunt battlefields.

He jumped out of bed and rushed to find the source of the noise, while his wife ran after him with the clothes he had forgotten to put on. They were met with a peculiar sight: a red woman riding in a chariot pulled by a one-legged horse. Beside the chariot was a man driving a cow.

Cú Chulainn told the man to stop, but the man said nothing. Cú Chulainn asked why the man didn't answer him, and the red woman said, "That is not a man." So he asked for the woman's name, and she shot back a bunch of scary words like "cold wind" and "cutting" and "terror," until he got angry and jumped on the chariot. But suddenly there was no chariot. Just an ominous black bird: the Badb.

## NEMAIN

Scholars don't know much about the third sister, Nemain. Her name means "panic," and by some accounts she warps soldiers' minds so much that they wind up killing their friends and allies. But until someone finds a better account of this goddess, that's really all we can say.

CÚ, YOUR CLOTHES!

# NATURE SPIRITS
## AND ELEMENTALS

THE FORCES OF THE NATURAL WORLD

Animism is the belief that plants, animals, places, and things have spirits of their own. It's a fundamental piece of most mythology, and the prehistoric foundation of many of the world's first religions. And while some later religions and myths moved away from the idea, it's never completely disappeared—you can still hear echoes of it in myths and folktales all over the world. Here are just a few well-known spirits of nature.

## ALFAR

The Alfar of Norse and Germanic folklore are the main inspiration for the elves you might find in fantasy stories today. Some accounts claim they live in a place called Alfheim, "Home of the Elves." Others say they are based in our world, hiding in forests, hills, and rocks. Sources also vary on their personalities and powers, but most agree that they are supernaturally beautiful, and powerful enough to be very helpful—or very dangerous.

## APSARAS

Apsaras are Buddhist and Hindu spirits of clouds and water. They take the form of gorgeous, well-dressed women who dance with more grace and precision than any human could. They often entertain the gods, accompanied by the music of part-bird spirits called ganharvas.

## DOMOVOI

In Slavic and Russian folklore, every home has a spirit called a domovoi. They usually take the form of tiny, hairy old men, but have been known to shape-shift into various animals or even the form of the human who owns the house. As long as he's kept happy, a domovoi is a good (if mischievous) protector of the home and family. If not, watch out—his pranks can turn vicious.

## DWARFS

The dwarfs of Norse mythology are not the dwarfs of fantasy novels. They are pitch-black creatures of incredible strength and skill, and despite the name, some are huge. They labor underground in mines and workshops, forging items of great power and beauty: magical weapons, jewelry, and armor. Some say they originated as the maggots that crawled in the dead body of the giant Ymir. Whether or not that's true, we know that they are not nice creatures. They are greedy and suspicious, and their chief concern is protecting their own stuff. If that means cursing a human or a god, so be it.

## FAIRIES

These days, fairies are usually depicted as cute little winged people, dancing on flowers. But those fairies are a recent invention, only a few centuries old. Their ancestors, the fairies of Celtic mythology, are not so harmless. They were the Tuatha Dé Danann, a proud and magical people who were driven out of Ireland by the first human settlers. At the end of that war, they retreated into the Otherworld, a separate, parallel realm. Some are kind, some are not, but all are dangerous. If you should ever meet a fairy, eat nothing, drink nothing, accept no gifts, and keep careful watch on your children—they have been known to steal them.

## KACHINAS

The Hopi people of the American Southwest honor gods and spirits called kachinas. They are both nature spirits and spirits of the dead, believed to live in the mountains and control the clouds and rain. Many Hopi ceremonies involve dressing up in kachina costumes, and kachina dolls were common Hopi toys. There are hundreds of individual kachinas.

## KAPRES

Kapres are Philippine tree spirits. They are hairy, bearded creatures that stand up to ten feet tall. They live in big trees and spend most of their time invisible, smoking on pipes. But beware: Kapres aren't nice spirits. They like tricking travelers and getting them lost.

## NĀGA

In the myths of South and Southeast Asia, a nāga is an intelligent snake spirit. The details vary depending on the specific tradition—they can be kind or malevolent, have human features or look entirely snakelike, and sometimes have wings or even extra heads. They appear in the great Hindu epic the *Mahabharata* as both enemies and allies of the gods. In some places, they are fertility deities; in others, nature spirits; and in still others, survivors of a long-gone undersea empire.

## NYMPHS

Greek myths are full of these beautiful nature spirits. They are typically related to natural objects like trees, streams, or grottoes, and if that object dies or disappears, so do they. Many myths mention water nymphs, or nereids, which are spirits of rivers and streams and daughters of two Titans named Okeanos and Tethys. But there are also oreids (mountain nymphs), auloniads (field nymphs), alseids (forest nymphs), and various other nymphs who represent individual plants. Some of the most famous nymphs accompany the goddess Artemis on her hunts.

## OBAKE

An obake is a shape-changing spirit of Japanese folklore. They come in many varieties, including kitsune (fox spirits), tanuki (raccoon dog spirits), bakeneko (cat spirits), and kodama (tree or plant spirits). Most of them are friendly but very fond of tricks.

## PATUPAIAREHE

The Maori of New Zealand tell tales of tiny, tricky, unnaturally pale-skinned spirits called patupaiarehe. They lurk deep in forests or high up on mountaintops, playing ethereal music on their flutes. Some say they are wandering spirits of the dead, never properly laid to rest.

## SATYRS

Satyrs are rural fertility spirits of Greek mythology. They are hairy, horned men from the waist up and goats from the waist down. They spend their days playing music (especially on flutes) and chasing nymphs around. In most cases, it's best to avoid them—there are many stories in which their playfulness turns to violence.

## VILAS

Vilas are Eastern European spirits of wind and rain. Sometimes they take the form of beautiful, long-haired women, but they also appear as swans, horses, wolves, and other animals. They are usually kind to humans, but they are fiercely protective of animals and have been known to use wind and storms to punish those who would do them harm.

# NJORD

## GOD OF SHIPS

# NJORD

**TRADITION:** Norse/Scandinavian
**HOME:** Noatán, the enclosure of ships

You can't talk about Vikings without talking about ships. Viking explorers sailed to North America centuries before Columbus, Viking traders carried goods across every major waterway in Europe, and Viking raiders looted and pillaged thousands of miles of coastlines. Viking fortunes rose and fell with the waves of the ocean, so it should come as no surprise that they had a god of ships. But it might surprise you to find out how little we actually know about him.

The Vikings didn't write much down, so even gods as important and widely worshipped as Njord are something of a mystery. We know Njord is a god of boats, the ocean, and seafaring in general. His command of the sea makes him a very wealthy god, and his favor can mean huge hauls for fishermen and huge profits for traders. We also know that he has something to do with fertility, and something to do with death.

Njord is officially a member of the Vanir clan of gods, but ever since the Aesir-Vanir War, he and his children, Freya and Freyr, have lived with the Aesir in Asgard. There were probably plenty of stories about him in Viking times, but since then we've lost all but one: the time Njord got married.

In addition to sacrificing animals in religious rituals, some ancient Norsemen sacrificed ships.

## NJORD'S NOT-SO-GREAT MARRIAGE

One day a giantess named Skadi arrived at Asgard, and she was very, very angry. The gods, she claimed, had killed her father Thjazi (they had), and now they had to make it right. She demanded two things: a god to be her husband, and someone to bring her joy. Odin granted her wishes, but with one caveat: She could only look at the gods' feet before she chose her new husband. Skadi figured the best-looking god, Baldr, would have the best feet and accepted the deal.

The gods all hid behind a screen that covered them from the ankles up, and Skadi found the most beautiful feet among them. But when the screen came down, she found that her new husband wasn't Baldr at all—it was Njord.

Now Skadi was in an even worse mood, and someone still needed to bring her joy. That task fell to Loki, who brought over a rope, an angry goat, and a story.

He told Skadi that earlier that day he had brought the goat to the market, but his hands were too full to hold the goat. So he tied one end of the rope to the goat's beard and the other to his own testicles. Skadi couldn't help but laugh as Loki acted out the story, flailing and squawking and tripping around as the goat struggled to escape.

But Skadi's joy couldn't last. Once Loki's story was done, Skadi and Njord left, and their marriage wasn't a happy one. Half the time, they lived at Njord's beachside home, but it was far too wet for Skadi. The other half, they lived on Skadi's mountain, but Njord couldn't stand the cold. Eventually they split up and went their separate ways.

## All Aboard the Death Boat

Death and ships were closely related in ancient Norse culture. Some graves were surrounded by stones placed in the shape of a boat. By 600 CE, some people were put to rest in actual boats, which would be lit on fire in the water or on land or even buried intact.

# NU GUA

## THE SNAKE-BODIED GODDESS OF RENEWAL

## NU GUA

**TRADITION:** Chinese
**HOME:** The Heavenly Realm
**ALSO KNOWN AS:** Nü Kua, Nuwa

Nu Gua has seen better days. In her time, she was a major deity, the goddess of creation and renewal. She is mentioned in books from 300 BCE and was likely worshipped for centuries before then. But times change, and Nu Gua has fallen from an exalted goddess to a relatively minor figure, with many of her powers and functions passing to her brother and/or husband, Fu Xi. Some sources even claim she was just a human. Here are the most interesting stories about Nu Gua the goddess and Nu Gua the human.

## NU GUA'S MUD-SHAKIN' PEOPLE-MAKIN'

A long, long time ago, Nu Gua came down from the heavens to live on Earth. Back then, Earth was mostly empty, and soon she was bored—and lonely. One day, she caught sight of her reflection in a stream, and a solution came to her: If she had company, she wouldn't be lonely. She decided to make some people.

Nu Gua grabbed some mud, molded it into a figure, and brought it to life. The creation jumped to its feet, dancing and singing and overjoyed to be alive. Nu Gua was happy, too, and used some more mud to make another, and then another.

Soon she had a whole crowd of people. But Nu Gua realized that she had to work a lot faster to fill up the whole world. So she took hold of a nearby vine, dipped it into the mud, and flicked it around in all directions. Droplets of mud flew everywhere, and each drop turned into another person.

Eventually the people got bored and wandered off to populate the earth. But Nu Gua didn't mind. As long as she could hear their voices, she was happy.

## NU GUA SAVES THE WORLD

Nu Gua may have made people, but she wasn't in charge of Earth. That honor belonged to the fire god, Zhu Rong. He was a good, wise emperor, respected by everyone—except for his son, the water god Gong Gong.

Hoping to replace his father, Gong Gong gathered an army of sea creatures to attack Zhu Rong's fortress. But the fire god was in charge for a reason, and in short order Gong Gong's army had been burned to a crisp.

Enraged at his defeat, Gong Gong threw the world's biggest temper tantrum. He stomped and thrashed and headbutted Mount Buzhou, causing it to collapse—along with the section of the sky it had been holding up. Without support, the whole sky tilted to the northwest, and the earth tilted to the southeast. Fires, floods, earthquakes, and sinkholes covered the world.

When Nu Gua saw the destruction, she selected some colorful stones from a riverbed, melted them together into a beautiful mix of colors, and used them to plug the holes in the sky. Next, she tracked down an enormous tortoise, killed it, and used its legs to prop up the heavens, saving the world from destruction. But she never got the world quite level, and that's why, ever since, the rivers in China flow toward the southeast.

## NU GUA RIDES A GOURD

In another legend, originating in southern China, Nu Gua isn't a goddess but a little girl.

A farmer was working in his fields one day when he heard distant thunder. He grabbed his pitchfork, ran back to his cottage, and opened the door of a huge iron cage. He had been waiting for this moment. As the rain began, he stood guard.

The next roar of thunder brought the thunder god himself, huge and frightening and wielding a giant ax. But the farmer was ready and stabbed the god with his pitchfork, pushed him into the cage, and locked the door. Just like that, the rain clouds cleared and the sun shone again.

The farmer went to town to buy herbs and a sauce to pickle the god. As he left, he warned his daughter and son that no matter what his prisoner said, they must not give him any water. But the kids felt sorry for the poor injured god and gave him some anyway. As soon as the water touched his lips, the thunder god recovered and burst free of the cage.

As thanks, he gave the children one of his teeth and told them to plant it if they wanted to live. They did as they were told, and the tooth sprouted before their eyes into the biggest gourd they had ever seen. As it grew, the weather changed— it started to rain, and it didn't stop.

When the farmer got home and saw what happened, he told his kids to climb into the gourd. He himself boarded a boat, and as the world flooded he floated to heaven to ask the gods for help. The emperor of heaven helped—a little too well. The flood rushed away in an instant, and the farmer's boat plummeted back to Earth, killing him. The gourd, however, bounced to safety, and the kids inside survived, grew up, and (with the gods' permission) repopulated the earth. From that point on, the brother was known as Fu Xi, "Bottle Gourd," and the sister as Nu Gua, another term for gourd or melon.

BOUNCE!

# ODIN

## THE ALL-FATHER

# ODIN

**TRADITION:** Norse
**HOME:** Asgard
**ALSO KNOWN AS:** Wotan (Germanic), Woden (Old English)

Odin (pronounced "Oh-din") is a very peculiar character. On the one hand, he's the god of Viking kings and the chief of his pantheon, and his power, magic, wisdom, and knowledge have changed the course of history. On the other hand, he's so crafty and treacherous that even his worshippers acknowledge that he can't be trusted.

Odin isn't terribly concerned with truth, justice, or rules, and is a well-known breaker of taboos—not least in his practice of *seidr*, a form of traditionally feminine magic that few Viking men would ever try. He can also sap willpower or inspire courage, change the course of battles, and speak with the dead.

Odin was the patron of many of the greatest Viking heroes, as well as more common berserkers, warrior-shamans who fought without armor and in some cases were said to transform into animals. Mostly, though, Odin is a god of the elite of Viking society, especially those who rule through cunning.

## ODIN'S SELF-SACRIFICE

The world tree, Yggdrasil, grows from a vast, dark pool of water called the Well of Urd. All sorts of mysterious powers and entities are hidden in its depths, including the knowledge of runes, a magical alphabet that can alter destiny itself.

Odin wanted this knowledge, but the runes only reveal themselves to those who prove themselves worthy. So to prove himself, Odin sacrificed himself. He hung himself by the neck from a branch of Yggdrasil, stabbed himself with his own spear, and gazed into the Well of Urd. After nine full days, the runes revealed themselves, and he learned to wound, to heal, to protect, to raise the dead, and to manipulate hearts and minds, along with a variety of other powers.

## HOW ODIN LOST HIS EYE

That wasn't the only time Odin suffered for wisdom—or even the only time he did it at a well. There was a god named Mímir who guarded a different well of knowledge. One day Odin arrived at Mímir's well and asked for a drink. Mímir agreed to give him one, but only if Odin traded one of his eyes for it.

Some folks might have walked away, but Odin always went to great lengths for knowledge. He poked out his eye, dropped it into the well, and took a drink, gladly trading sight for insight.

THIS HAD BETTER BE GOOD.

## ODIN STEALS POETRY

In Norse mythology, the source of all artistic talent and inspiration is the Mead of Poetry. (Mead is a drink made of fermented honey.) But this magical drink wasn't always available to mankind, or even to the gods. Long ago, it was owned by a giant named Suttung, and Odin wanted it.

First Odin disguised himself as a mortal and sought out Suttung's brother, Baugi. Then he killed all of Baugi's servants and offered to serve Baugi himself in exchange for some of Suttung's mead. Odin did the work and asked for his reward, and Baugi in turn asked Suttung for some mead to pay the disguised Odin. Suttung refused.

But now Odin had an idea of where the special mead was hidden, and he got Baugi to dig a hole in a nearby mountain. When Odin crawled through, he found the mead, but he also found Suttung's daughter, Gunnlod. He bargained with her until she agreed to give him three sips. Then he took the three most enormous sips he could, downing a vat with each one, and turned into an eagle to make his escape.

Suttung chased him as he flew, and though Odin made it back to Asgard, he lost a bit of the mead on the way. The drops of mead that fell to earth granted mortals the power of poetry.

# OKUNINUSHI

**HERO OF IZUMO**

# OKUNINUSHI

**TRADITION:** Japanese/Shinto
**HOME:** Izumo, Japan
**ALSO KNOWN AS:** Ōkuninushi no Mikoto

Okuninushi is the hero of Japan—or, at least, the hero of Izumo, a small region of Japan whose mythology would later spread across most of the country. He had a relatively humble childhood, but with compassion, wit, and luck, he rose to become a king, a god's son-in-law, and ultimately a god himself.

## THE WHITE RABBIT

Okuninushi was one of eighty-one brothers, all of whom hoped to marry the beautiful princess of Inaba. They set off for her father's palace, walking one by one in a line stretching over the horizon. The strongest brothers fought for positions at the front of the line. Okuninushi traveled alone, all the way at the back.

On the way, the brothers came across a rabbit on the side of the road. It was completely hairless and squeaking in pain. They suggested the rabbit bathe in salt water, but that only made the pain worse.

When Okuninushi arrived, he asked the rabbit what was wrong. The rabbit replied that he had been on an island but wanted to travel to Izumo. Since there was no bridge, he convinced some crocodiles to float in a line and form a bridge for him to hop across. In return, he agreed to count them all and tell them whether there were more of them than there were creatures in the ocean. He was nearly across when he let it slip that he had tricked the crocodiles. So, they attacked him and bit his skin off.

Okuninushi told the rabbit to go to the mouth of a river, wash in its water, and then roll around in pollen and grass. The rabbit tried it, and his fur regrew. Healed and happy, he revealed himself to be a god, and as a reward, he made sure that Okuninushi, not his brothers, would get to marry the princess—and so he did.

## THE UNDERWORLD'S WORST FATHER-IN-LAW

Okuninushi and his new bride were very happy, but his brothers weren't. They plotted to kill him, and on a few occasions even succeeded—once by crushing him with a tree and once by tricking him into catching a huge burning boulder. But Okuninushi's mom had a good relationship with the gods, and each time she managed to get him resurrected.

Okuninushi was sick of dying and decided to ask his ancestor, the powerful god Susanoo, for advice. But not long after he arrived in Susanoo's palace in the underworld, he met Susanoo's daughter, the beautiful Suseri-hime. They fell in love and got married in secret.

When Susanoo found out, he fumed with anger, but he didn't let his fury show. Instead, he made a big performance of accepting his new son-in-law. He offered Okuninushi a beautiful room in his palace, with a bed that was as comfortable as it was full of deadly snakes. But Suseri-hime predicted the trick and gave Okuninushi a magical scarf to protect him.

When he saw Okuninushi unharmed, Susanoo granted him a better room, full of killer centipedes, but Okuninushi's scarf kept him safe once again. So Susanoo granted him an even *better* room, this time full of stinging bees, but the scarf protected him from those, too.

Beds full of creepy-crawlies weren't working, so Susanoo tried something bolder. He sent Okuninushi into a field to retrieve an arrow and lit the field on fire. But to Susanoo's surprise, that didn't work, either. A friendly field mouse showed Okuninushi how to hide from the flames, and got him the arrow, to boot. When Okuninushi returned with the arrow, Susanoo was so impressed that he stopped trying to kill him for a while.

Okuninushi, meanwhile, planned his escape. His chance came when he found Susanoo asleep in his bath. Okuninushi sneaked up, tied Susanoo's hair to the ceiling rafters, stole a sword and bow, grabbed Suseri-hime, and ran. When Susanoo woke up, he shook himself loose (knocking down the building in the process), found another bow, and gave chase. He quickly reached shooting distance, drew an arrow, pulled, aimed, and . . . decided to let them go. Instead of shooting, he shouted the advice that Okuninushi had come for in the first place: With the bow and sword he had stolen, Okuninushi could defeat his eighty brothers and rule Izumo.

And it worked—Okuninushi became king of Izumo and went on to invent medicine and found a whole noble family. Some time later, he gave his kingdom to the goddess Amaterasu in exchange for godhood.

# OSIRIS

## THE DEAD GOD

# OSIRIS

**TRADITION:** Egyptian
**HOME:** Duat
**ALSO KNOWN AS:** Usir

Ancient Egyptians had really elaborate funerals. People spent fortunes building tombs for themselves and filled them with treasures, tools, pets, and servants (who weren't always dead before burial). Once they died, their bodies were preserved using the most advanced science of the day. Meanwhile, their souls traveled to the underworld, through the great gates, and past all sorts of spirits until they arrived at the court of its king, Osiris.

Osiris is the god of death, dead people, and especially dead pharaohs. It isn't totally clear where his earliest worshippers lived, but by 2500 BCE, he had worshippers all over Egypt. Osiris is also a god of life and fertility—according to one myth, plants only grow when he puts life into the ground. Some myths even claim that all water starts as his bodily fluids, although some river gods might disagree.

It is probably worth noting, at this point, that Osiris is dead.

## HOW OSIRIS GOT DEAD

Osiris didn't start out dead. He came out of his mother alive and wearing a crown. He was chosen to succeed the god Geb as pharaoh of the gods, and by all accounts his reign was peaceful and prosperous. But all was not perfect. His brother, Seth, wanted the throne and plotted to take it from Osiris.

Well, "plotted" might be a little too generous. It wasn't a very smart plot. Seth just waited until Osiris was alone and then (depending on the source) beat him up, trampled him, or drowned him.

Then Seth cut Osiris's body up into little pieces and hid them all over Egypt. When he was done, Seth returned to the kingdom of the gods and declared that, as the dead king's brother, he would be the next pharaoh.

## Geb, Nut, Shu, and This Strange Gymnastic Tomb Painting

A lot of Egyptian tombs show an image like this one. It depicts one of the most important moments in Egyptian myth: the separation of the sky from the earth. From top to bottom, the gods depicted are Nut, goddess of the sky; Shu, god of air; and Geb, god of the earth. The story goes like this:

Geb and Nut were Shu's kids, and they loved each other—really, really loved each other, more than brothers and sisters are supposed to love each other. Shu didn't like this, so he shoved his way in between them and held Nut up and Geb down, forever separated. And since Shu, Nut, and Geb were really the air, sky, and earth, this really meant that the air shoved its way in and held the sky up above the earth.

Incidentally, Geb and Nut's kids— Osiris, Isis, Nephthys, and Seth—all wound up marrying each other, too.

## HOW OSIRIS GOT UNDEAD

Osiris's wife, Isis, was beside herself with grief. She and her sister traveled across all of Egypt searching for Osiris's scattered body parts. When they found them all, Isis used her powerful magic to revive him. It didn't work for long—he died again shortly after—but it was long enough for Isis to get pregnant with a son, Horus.

Osiris was embalmed and mummified. But the gods agreed that his death was undeserved and gave Osiris a special privilege: His spirit would leave his decaying body and become the king of the underworld. From then on, when folks died, their souls would travel to Osiris's court to be weighed against a divine feather. If they had led righteous lives, their souls were light as that feather and they were granted an afterlife in Osiris's domain. If, on the other hand, they had been unrighteous, they were obliterated.

Depending on the account, Osiris's body was split into anywhere between fourteen and forty-two parts, and numerous ancient temples claimed to hold pieces of Osiris.

# PARVATI

## GODDESS OF DEVOTION

# PARVATI

**TRADITION:** Indian/Hindu
**HOME:** Mount Kailash
**ALSO KNOWN AS:** Devi, Shakti, Uma, Durga, Kali (all incarnations and/or forms)

Of all the great Hindu goddess Devi's incarnations, the most popular might be Parvati, goddess of love and devotion. She is the loyal, caring, oh-so-beautiful wife of Shiva, one of Hinduism's top gods. She's also the only one in the entire Hindu pantheon who can consistently change Shiva's mind about things like killing someone, or resurrecting someone, or withdrawing from the world to meditate forever. Most stories about Parvati are really stories about her relationship with Shiva.

## PARVATI'S PREINCARNATION

The Hindu idea of reincarnation—that after death, you are reborn in another form—applies to gods, too. In her most recent life, Parvati was a goddess named Sati. More than anything in the world, Sati wanted to marry Shiva. Her father, Daksha, however, didn't approve, and if you look at it from his perspective, it makes sense. Shiva might have been an important, powerful god, but he was also a dirty hermit with matted hair who lived alone on a mountain.

Daksha arranged a party to find a suitable husband for Sati and invited every single god except Shiva. But Sati didn't want another god. She wanted Shiva. She focused all of her energy on that desire, so strongly that Shiva felt it, miles away. When Sati threw up a garland of flowers for her suitors to catch, Shiva appeared and took it from the air. They were married soon after.

Later, Daksha threw another party for a grand sacrifice, and again invited every single god except Shiva. Sati was hurt. She knew her father disapproved, but surely now that they were married, Shiva at least deserved an invitation. She traveled to Daksha's home to confront him, but he was unmoved. Not only did he still hate Shiva, but now he thought Sati was tarnished for having married him.

PLEASE BE SHIVA.
PLEASE BE SHIVA.
PLEASE BE SHIVA...

## Devi

Depending how you look at it, there could be countless Hindu goddesses or there could be only one. The most common interpretation is somewhere in between: a whole lot of goddesses who are also aspects, versions, or incarnations of the one goddess. That goddess is usually called Devi, which means "goddess," or Shakti, which means "power."

There's a whole branch of modern Hinduism, called Shaktism, in which Devi is the most important deity. But since myths about Devi herself are rarer than myths about her various incarnations, in this book some of them are listed in their own chapters.

Sati tried to reason with her father, but nothing would convince him. Finally, she reached her limit. She cursed Daksha, swearing that he would die at Shiva's hands and that she would be reincarnated as Shiva's next wife. And then she threw herself into the sacrificial flames and died.

Shiva felt it as soon as it happened and charged into Daksha's home in a mad fury. He fought back all the assembled gods, chopped off Daksha's head, and then gently, sadly, lifted Sati's burned body from the fire. He carried it out with him and did a dance of grief all across the world.

YOU RANG?

## SATI'S REINCARNATION

Shiva wandered the world for ages in mourning. But nothing lasts forever, and eventually he returned home and settled into a life of quiet meditation. Serving him was a beautiful local girl named Parvati. Just like Sati, Parvati dreamed of marrying Shiva. She even heard a prophecy that someday she would. But as time passed, she began to lose hope. No matter what she tried, Shiva just kept meditating. The love god, Kama, tried to help, but even his flower-tipped love arrows only roused Shiva for a few minutes. Shiva vaporized Kama, and soon enough he was back to meditating.

Parvati decided that if her looks and personality didn't do it for Shiva, maybe religious suffering would. So she left Shiva and meditated, starved herself, froze herself, lived alone, and slept on nothing but rocks. And she kept on doing it, day after day, week after week, year after year.

One day, a traveling priest stumbled into Parvati and asked why she was putting herself through so much suffering. When she said she wanted to marry Shiva, the priest scoffed. Shiva, he said, was a smelly old bum. Parvati said she loved him anyway. Then the priest called Shiva a scary guy with a horrible temper who sneaks around graveyards. Parvati argued for a while and then simply covered her ears, refusing to hear any more. And then, just like that, the priest was gone and Shiva stood in his place. He was moved by Parvati's devotion to him. When he asked her to marry him, she said yes.

Don't be too worried about Daksha. He came back to life. But in place of his original head, Shiva gave him a goat's.

# PELE

## FIERY VOLCANO GODDESS

# PELE

**TRADITION:** Hawaiian
**HOME:** Halema'uma'u Crater, Hawaii

Volcanoes are pretty rare, and volcano gods are even rarer. But the island of Hawaii is made of volcanoes, so it should come as no surprise that its most famous deity, Pele, is a volcano goddess.

Pele is much like the volcanoes she represents: beautiful, powerful, and warm, but there's always a chance that she will turn nasty. She has a fiery temper, and when she blows her top, everything burns.

## HOW PELE GOT TO HAWAII

Most myths agree that Pele wasn't native to Hawaii, but they disagree on how and why she wound up there. Some stories blame Pele's sister, a sea goddess, who was afraid of Pele's ambition and chased her off their original island and across the ocean. Others say that Pele had an affair with her sister's husband. Either way, Pele fled, and her sister chased her from island to island, snuffing out all the new volcanoes Pele made with waves of ocean water.

Time after time, Pele escaped, until her sister finally caught her in Hawaii. Pele was killed, but though her body was destroyed, her spirit wasn't. It emerged, flaming and pure, far more powerful than ever before. She set up a home in one of Hawaii's volcanic craters and has lived there ever since.

## PELE AND THE MAN-PIG

In ancient times, the Hawaiian islands were home to all sorts of gods and spirits. One of the greatest was Kama-puaa, who could transform at will from a handsome man to a big, fat, angry hog.

LEARN. SOME. MANNERS.

QUIT BEIN' SUCH A HOTHEAD.

SCRATCH SCRATCH

One day, Kama-puaa wandered past a cliff overlooking Pele's molten home. One of Pele's sisters noticed him up there in his form as a dashing young man. She pointed him out to the rest of her sisters, and soon they were all asking Pele if they could invite him down. But Pele refused. She said it wasn't a man up there at all, but a stupid, ugly pig—and then she told Kama-puaa that directly.

Kama-puaa responded with insults of his own, and soon they began a shouting match, insults giving way to threats. Pele tried to scare him off with blasts of smoke and lava, but Kama-puaa didn't budge.

Finally Pele agreed to her sisters' demands and invited Kama-puaa down to join them. But their relationship didn't improve. Pele was disgusted by Kama-puaa's piggishness, and Kama-puaa couldn't handle Pele's fierce temper. It wasn't long until their sniping gave way to violence.

Pele threw the first blow, a blast of scalding lava, but Kama-puaa deflected it with seawater. Then he sent more water into her fire pit, causing explosions of steam and lava that shook the whole island. As the water poured in, the fire pit began to cool. Pele added lava as fast as she could, but not fast enough. Soon the fire pit was cold and black, and Pele was drowning.

Pele called to the gods of the underworld for help, and they sent her some of their power. A spark appeared, and then a

Some people say Pele misses Kama-puaa. It's said that her favorite sacrifices are the sorts of creatures Kama-puaa would turn into: black pigs and thick-skinned fish, among other things.

fire, and then torrents of lava filled the pit and streamed out toward Kama-puaa. His hair and skin burned as he fled through the fire, down to the shore, and into the sea. He turned into a thick-skinned fish, and some native Hawaiians swear that if you listen closely, you can still hear it snorting.

# PERUN

## MYSTERIOUS SLAVIC GOD OF THUNDER

# PERUN

**TRADITION:** Slavic

**HOME:** Parv

**ALSO KNOWN AS:** Perkunas (Lithuanian), Piorun (Polish)

Perun probably wasn't too mysterious to his worshippers, but he is very mysterious to us. We know he was one of the most popular and widely worshipped gods in what is now Eastern Europe, especially among warriors. We know that he is a god of thunder and war. And we know that he defends the home of the gods with his ax and bow and rides a flaming chariot across the sky.

Other than that? It's hard to say. The ancient Slavs didn't have a written language. However, there is one Perun myth that scholars are pretty sure about: the battles between Perun and his archnemesis, Veles.

## THE ETERNAL BATTLES OF PERUN AND VELES

Veles (or Volos) is, as far as we can tell, the opposite of Perun. He's an earth god, an animal god, and a god of death and commerce. While Perun lives in the highest reaches of Parv, the world tree, Veles lives in the roots at its base.

Every year, in the form of a giant snake, Veles slithers up the world tree and steals Perun's cows. Then he flees, while Perun chases him around and shoots lightning from the sky. When lightning strikes earth, the legends say, it's because Veles was just hiding in that spot.

SLITHER SLITHER

Eventually, after a long battle, Perun chases Veles all the way back to the underworld, recovers his cattle, and either slays Veles or just yells at him and leaves. But each year, sure as the seasons, Veles comes back to steal again.

The most common interpretation of this myth says that it's about the seasons. Perun is a god of dry heat and Veles is a god of cold wetness, and as both of them climb or descend the world tree, the seasons change.

But there are other versions, too, and other interpretations. In one, Veles steals Perun's wife, the sun, every evening, and Perun rescues her

## How We Know What We Know About Slavic Mythology

Primary sources on Slavic mythology are incredibly rare, mostly because the Slavs didn't write things down. As a result, most Slavic myths are partly invented, based on the information scholars are able to piece together from what they do have, including:

- **Non-Slavic historical records:** Some Byzantine treaties and records mention a few Slavic gods' names, and a twelfth-century Danish historian named Saxo Grammaticus went into some detail describing the Slavic temples and cities that the Danes conquered.

- **Writings by Christian missionaries:** There are more of these, but they aren't as trustworthy, because the authors were trying to stamp out the local Slavic religions and often didn't speak the local languages well enough to understand them.

- **Old calendars and holidays:** Many holidays celebrated by ancient peasants were related to the gods.

- **Songs, poems, and folk beliefs:** Most of these weren't written down until centuries after Slavic lands had turned Christian, but scholars can find echoes of ancient beliefs buried in them.

- **Comparative mythology:** Myths have a way of traveling, and there are a lot of similarities between some Slavic, Lithuanian, and Baltic myths.

- **Archeology:** Every time someone unearths another ancient shrine or statue, we learn a little more about the people who made them.

every morning. Some even say that Perun and Veles are both husbands of the sun and are locked in an endless battle over who gets to be with her and when.

## POST-CHRISTIAN PERUN

Some parts of Slavic paganism lasted long after the region's official conversion to Christianity. Gods, rituals, and holidays weren't replaced so much as mixed into the new beliefs. Perun's name disappeared, but much of his personality, powers, and role in people's lives transferred to the Christian saint Elijah, who had a similar habit of throwing sky-fire at people who displeased him.

The Lithuanian version of Perun, Perkunas, once punished the moon by breaking his face. That's why the moon goes from full to new every couple of weeks or so.

C'MON, GUYS, IT'S SAINT ELIJAH!

# POSEIDON

SAVAGE GOD OF THE SEA

## POSEIDON

**TRADITION:** Greek/Roman
**HOME:** Mount Olympus/Under the sea
**ALSO KNOWN AS:** Neptune (Roman)

If you look at a map of ancient Greece, you might notice that there's a whole lot of water. It's no accident that most of the empires of the ancient world (and today, for that matter) sat on rivers and seas. Waterways are good for food, trade, defense, and communication, among other things. If your country is built on coasts and islands, it pays to keep the sea god happy. And if your sea god is also the god of earthquakes? Better hope he's an easygoing god.

Poseidon is not an easygoing god. He's wild and violent, untamed and savage. While he's quick to defend allies and generous to those he deems worthy, he spends most of his time getting into fights and attacking women.

## POSEIDON BECOMES A SHEEP, ATTACKS A WOMAN

Long ago, in the land of Thrace, there lived Theophane, a girl so beautiful that everybody wanted to marry her. No matter how many guys she rejected, more showed up to try their luck. As it turned out, Poseidon wanted her, too. He appeared to her, grabbed her, and carried her off to an island called Crumissa.

Theophane's suitors were more persistent than Poseidon had expected. Once they realized what had happened, they tracked her down and chartered a ship to take them to Crumissa. They arrived on the island, excited to get back to fighting over the bride-to-be. But try as they might, they couldn't find her. In fact, they couldn't find anybody at all—just a big herd of sheep. Depressed and defeated, they boarded their ship and returned home.

But Theophane had been there all along. When Poseidon saw the suitors coming, he turned her, himself, and everyone else unlucky enough to live on Crumissa into sheep. Eventually, Theophane gave birth to a lamb with golden fleece, which starred in a later myth as the treasure sought by the hero Jason.

## POSEIDON BECOMES A HORSE, ATTACKS A WOMAN

Demeter, goddess of agriculture, was already having a bad time, what with her daughter Persephone getting kidnapped by Hades. But nothing is so bad that it can't get worse—so, naturally, Poseidon showed up, full of desire. Demeter turned into a mare and fled, so Poseidon turned into a stallion and gave chase. Demeter was fast, but Poseidon was faster (he's the guy who invented horses, after all), and he caught her.

Demeter later gave birth to Despoina, a goddess, and Areion, a talking horse. The experience scarred Demeter, and she took to wearing black and hid herself in a cave. She stayed there, refusing to come out, and her absence caused crops to wither and people to starve. After some long talks with Pan, god of the wilds, and the Fates, she returned to the world, but she never forgave Poseidon.

### The Fates

Of all the characters in Greek myth, there are few with such great power and responsibility as the Fates. They are the keepers of the threads of life, one for each person on Earth. When a baby is born, the Fates spin a thread to represent that baby's entire life—its growth into a child and an adult, its choices, and eventually its death. A person's destiny isn't completely fixed, and the Fates leave room for a person's actions to change. But when their scissors slice a string of life, that life will end. The three Fates are:

- **Clotho,** who spins the thread of life
- **Lachesis,** who measures it
- **Atropos,** who cuts it

## POSEIDON REMAINS HIMSELF, ATTACKS A WOMAN

Long before Perseus grabbed her by the snake-hair and cut off her head, Medusa was just a run-of-the-mill, staggeringly beautiful human woman who served as a priestess of Athena. One day, while she was going about her duties in Athena's temple, Poseidon showed up and attacked her.

Poseidon had a lot of kids. In addition to human babies, he fathered monsters, mermaids, a cyclops, and whole barnyards' worth of animals.

You might expect Athena to have punished Poseidon, but the ancient Greeks had a different view on things. Instead, Athena punished Medusa, turning her hair into snakes and making it so anyone who ever looked at her would turn to stone.

Then again, older versions of the Medusa story say she was just born like that, so who knows?

# QUETZALCOATL

THE FEATHERED SERPENT

# QUETZALCOATL

**TRADITION:** Mesoamerican
**HOME:** Beyond the ocean
**ALSO KNOWN AS:** Kukulcán (Mayan)

The Aztecs believed that the earth and sky are connected, and that this connection is maintained by Quetzalcoatl (pronounced "*ket*-sal-kwat-l"), one of the most important gods of Mesoamerica.

Quetzalcoatl is an ancient god of the sky, wind, and rain. He was worshipped by the Aztecs and at least a thousand years of people who came before them. His priests were the most important in the Aztec religion, and he is (as far as we know) the only Mesoamerican god to have been incarnated as a human. He and his less friendly brother, Tezcatlipoca, have each made and destroyed the world several times. And according to one myth, Quetzalcoatl even created humanity— or, at least, the current version.

EH? EH?

## QUETZALCOATL MAKES HUMANS— OR, AT LEAST, THE CURRENT VERSION

After the destruction of the fourth world and the creation of the fifth, Quetzalcoatl went in search of the human remains he needed to make a new race of people (the previous race had all turned into fish). The only human bones left, though, were in the underworld, protected by the skull-faced death god, Mictlantecuhtli.

Mictlantecuhtli agreed to give the bones to Quetzalcoatl on one condition: Quetzalcoatl had to travel around the underworld four times while playing a conch shell trumpet. There was just one problem: The shell Mictlantecuhtli gave him had no holes. Quetzalcoatl assembled worms to drill holes in the shell and bees to fly around in it to make noise as he made his four rounds.

Mictlantecuhtli, true to his word, gave him the bones. Quetzalcoatl carried them to the other gods, and together they ground them up into a powder and mixed it with some of their divine blood. That bone-blood mixture became the new world's first people.

Most Aztec gods have a *nahualli*, an animal they are associated with. Quetzalcoatl's *nahualli* is a beautiful green bird called a quetzal.

## THE GOOD KING TOPILTZIN

It's not always clear which myths, if any, are based on history, especially when most of the sources got burned up in the 1500s. Take, for instance, Topiltzin, priest-king of the city of Tula, who was linked to a historical line of Toltec priest-kings and said to be an incarnation of Quetzalcoatl.

The legend says that despite his wise rulership, Topiltzin's reign was undermined by support for the rival god Black Tezcatlipoca. Topiltzin did all he could, but his subjects abandoned him in droves.

In one version of the story, Topiltzin accepted defeat and burned himself to death on a pyre. His heart rose up to become the morning star (which we know today as Venus).

Another version says that Topiltzin sailed east across the ocean, vowing to return one day to establish a golden era of peace and prosperity. This last version would provide the basis for one of history's greatest coincidences and play a role in the end of the Aztec nation.

## HERNÁN CORTÉS, THE COINCIDENTAL CONQUEROR

In 1519, a bunch of Spanish soldiers led by Hernán Cortés landed on the Aztecs' eastern shore in ships larger than the Aztecs had ever seen. To the Aztecs, these foreigners seemed to have supernaturally pale skin. They wore shining helmets and armor and rode enormous four-legged beasts. At a loss to explain what they were seeing, some of the Aztecs (including their king) argued that this might be Quetzalcoatl, returning as promised. It only added to their confusion when the Spanish missionaries, dressed a little like Aztec priests, kept talking about a god who died and came back to life. What's more, Cortés arrived in the capital, Tenochtitlán, on the exact day that Quetzalcoatl was prophesied to return.

The Aztecs eventually figured out that Cortés wasn't a returned god. But that didn't save them. Between Spanish plagues, Spanish soldiers, and all the famines and disasters that followed, the Aztec nation didn't last much longer. But still—it was some coincidence.

# RA

## THE FIRST PHARAOH OF THE GODS

## RA

**TRADITION:** Egyptian
**HOME:** The solar barque
**ALSO KNOWN AS:** Re

For most of ancient Egypt's history, the top god was a sun god. Sometimes that god was Ra. Sometimes it was a fusion of Ra and another sun god—Atum-Ra or Ra-Horakhty, for instance. But in one form or another, Ra was worshipped for thousands of years, even as most of Egypt converted to Christianity in the third and fourth centuries CE.

Ra is wise, strong, and brave, qualities that suited him well as the first pharaoh of the gods. He wields the power of the sun, the light, and life itself. He alone has access to the universe's most powerful magic—the power to die and be reborn. And thank goodness he does, because if he weren't reborn every morning to make his journey across the sky, the sun wouldn't rise and the world as we know it would end.

## THE TIME RA KILLED EVERYONE

At first, things were fine. The universe had been created, and everyone in it understood and respected its laws and its ruler, Ra. But as time went on, things began to change, and one day Ra discovered that the people of Earth were rejecting his rule and plotting to overthrow him.

Stunned, angered, and saddened, Ra summoned the other gods to advise him: Nun, the goddess of the abyss; Hathor, the goddess of joy and love; and Ra's children and grandchildren. They discussed and debated and eventually agreed that Ra should destroy humanity.

Ra turned Hathor into Sekhmet, a huge, wild lioness, and let her loose on Earth. In a frenzy, Sekhmet cut a swath of destruction across the world, killing and devouring everything she could find. As the world filled with blood, she got even more excited, because rolling around in pools of blood was Sekhmet's favorite thing.

As Ra gazed down on the carnage from his home in the sky he felt even more depressed. He tried to call the whole thing off and save what remained of humanity, but Sekhmet wouldn't listen. So Ra contacted humanity directly and offered them a way out.

Per Ra's instructions, the surviving humans filled seven thousand jugs with beer, dyed it all red, poured it on the ground and hid. Soon Sekhmet came along and, mistaking the red liquid for more blood, guzzled it down. By the time she was done, Sekhmet was too drunk to remember which way was up, much less who she wanted to kill. She fell asleep and transformed back into Hathor, and humanity (or what was left of it) was saved.

But while the worst was over, the fact remained: Humanity had plotted against Ra. And Ra has never forgotten. Since then, he has continued his daily journey across the sky and through the underworld and made sure to keep the cosmos running. But while the other gods may busy themselves with humans, Ra forever keeps his distance.

## ALL ABOARD THE SUN BOAT

Egyptian mythology has two stories about how the sun circles the earth, and both center on Ra.

In one version, Ra himself is the sun. He travels across the sky and dies at sunset, only to be reborn the next morning from a sky goddess.

In another version, Ra guides the solar barque, which is a kind of boat. At sunset, the barque passes beneath the horizon and begins a journey through the underworld. Along the way, Ra encounters demons and gods, the spirits of the dead, and the tortured souls of those who led less-than-righteous lives. Eventually, he unites with the god of the underworld himself, Osiris.

When morning comes, the two separate. Osiris stays behind while Ra sails up toward the dawn. All the while Ra is pursued and attacked by the forces of chaos, foremost among them Apep (or Apophis), an enormous snake that existed before time itself.

Luckily, Ra isn't the only one on the barque. He is accompanied by a bunch of other gods and goddesses who help to protect him, including Seth, the strongest of the gods, who stands at the front of the boat, spear raised and ready for Apep's next attack.

# RAMA

## HERO OF THE RAMAYANA

# RAMA

**TRADITION:** Indian/Hindu
**HOME:** The city of Ayodhya
**ALSO KNOWN AS:** Ramachandra

**R**ama is a paragon of Hindu virtues. He is good, just, and wise, mindful of his role and duties, respectful of his elders, loyal to his family, and strong and dedicated enough to protect them all. His story is recorded in one of the great Hindu epics, the *Ramayana*.

The *Ramayana* is long—twenty-four thousand verses long, to be exact—and full of love and conflict. While most of the story is clearly myth, there is some evidence that Rama might be loosely based on an actual guy who lived sometime before 700 BCE. Over a few centuries of retelling, his story gained more and more mythological elements, until by 200 CE he had become a blue-skinned, demon-slaying avatar of Vishnu.

## RAMA BECOMES A PRINCE

The gods were in trouble. The demon king Ravana was on a rampage, and neither gods nor demons could harm him. It was Vishnu, the Preserver, who finally came up with a solution: If Ravana was immune to gods, then the gods had to become mortals to defeat him. The gods all went down to be incarnated on Earth. Most of them became monkeys, but Vishnu divided his essence into four human princes, including our hero, Rama.

When Rama was sixteen, he visited a neighboring kingdom and saw the king's prized possession: a huge, impossibly strong bow that had once belonged to the god Shiva. The king, Dasaratha, offered the hand of his daughter, Sita, to anyone who could draw the bowstring, and although many had tried, no one ever managed it—until Rama arrived. He hardly broke a sweat as he drew the string so far back that the bow itself snapped in half. He and Sita were married soon after.

## RAMA BECOMES AN EXILE

Rama may have been first in line for King Dasaratha's throne, but the king had other wives and other sons. One of those wives tricked the king into naming her son, Bharata, as his heir and banishing Rama for fourteen years.

Rama left peacefully, joined by his wife, Sita, and his brother, Lakshmana. The king died of grief a few days later. When Bharata, who had been traveling, returned and discovered what had happened, he was outraged at the injustice. He rushed to catch Rama and offer him the kingship, but Rama refused. Though it pained him to leave his home, he chose to suffer rather than disobey the king's orders. And so Bharata returned to the palace to rule as well as he could.

Thirteen years later, Rama, Sita, and Lakshmana had traveled the world, slain some demons, and settled into a quiet life as forest hermits. One day, a passing demon named Shurpanakha happened upon them and fell in love with Rama. She disguised herself as a gorgeous woman and tried to seduce him. But Rama was faithful to his wife and rejected the demon. When the demon tried her luck with Lakshmana, she was rejected again. And when she got angry and attacked Sita, Rama and Lakshmana shot arrows through her nose and ears.

Shurpanakha went home and told her brother Khara what had happened. Furious, Khara brought his army of fourteen thousand demons to attack the forest. Rama killed them all. So Shurpanakha went to her even bigger brother, Ravana, whom you might remember from the beginning of this story.

Since attacking Rama directly hadn't worked out, Ravana came up with a new plan. He had one

of his demons disguise himself as a deer and lure Rama away on a hunt. Then, that same demon mimicked Rama's voice to lure Lakshmana away, too. And that left no one to stop Ravana from sneaking in and kidnapping Sita.

When they saw through the trick, Rama and Lakshmana raced back home, but they were too late. Sita was gone. So they set out after the demon king, fighting battles along the way, and eventually gaining help from the monkey king Sugriva and his massive monkey army.

They tracked down Ravana to his island kingdom and laid siege to his fortress. After three days of intense battling, Rama broke Ravana's heart—literally—and the rest of Ravana's army fled. Rama and Sita were finally reunited, just in time for the end of Rama's exile.

## RAMA BECOMES A KING

At long last, they all returned home. Rama was crowned king and Sita his queen. But false rumors trailed after them. Sita had been in Ravana's castle for a long time, they said. Maybe she hadn't been faithful to Rama after all? The rumors grew louder and louder, until Rama felt he had no choice but to give in to the demands of his people and exile Sita.

Years later, Rama sent messengers to Sita, asking her to return and swear her innocence. But Sita refused. She had faithfully followed Rama into exile, faithfully resisted Ravana while kidnapped, faithfully rejoiced when Rama rescued her, and faithfully gone into exile again. And Rama still doubted her? Sita asked the earth to reclaim her, and it swallowed her whole.

Rama didn't take the news well. He quit being king and spent the rest of his life in mourning. Years later, he died. As he ascended to the heavens and became Vishnu once again, he caught sight of Sita, waiting for him. "Sita," it turned out, had been Vishnu's wife, Lakshmi, and now that they were gods again, they could spend eternity together.

YEAH, I'M DONE.

# RAVEN

## THE CACKLING CREATOR

## RAVEN

**TRADITION:** Northwestern North American/Siberian

Traditionally, the Pacific Northwest (ranging from modern-day California up through Alaska and eastern Siberia) never had a dominant religion. There were a wide variety of cultures, from settled tribes in Oregon and Washington to nomadic bands in the Arctic Circle, and a wide variety of myths to match. But one character shows up all over the region: Raven. Sometimes he's a creator god, sometimes he's a trickster, but he is always powerful, clever, unpredictable, and lazy.

PBBPRRT

## HOW RAVEN FINALLY GOT AROUND TO MAKING THE WORLD

According to the Chukchi people of Siberia, long before the world existed, Raven lived with his wife in a tiny, boring space. One day his wife asked him to create a world so she wouldn't be so bored all the time. But Raven claimed he couldn't. So she decided to create something herself and went to sleep.

As she slept, she lost her feathers and grew big and fat, and before she woke she gave birth to two strange, featherless twins—the first people. When the twins saw Raven, they both cracked up, laughing at his feathers and squawking voice, but their mom told them to stop making fun of Dad.

Raven didn't like being shown up, so he decided to create something, too. He flew outside their home, way up high, and started pooping. Wherever his droppings landed, they became mountains and lakes and valleys and rivers. Then he made plants and animals for people to eat as they spread across the earth.

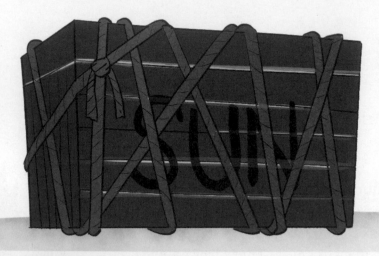

## HOW RAVEN STOLE THE SUN

Raven didn't make the sun. It existed long before he did, but it was hidden away by a sun-hoarding jerk who wanted it all for himself. According to the Tlingit people in Alaska, Raven is the one who released it.

The man who kept the sun lived in a hut with his daughter and carefully guarded his treasure so that no one would steal it. So Raven found another way in: He used his magic to impregnate the sun hoarder's daughter with himself. Raven grew inside her and eventually was born in the form of a baby boy. From the moment of his birth, baby-Raven cried and pointed at the light-filled bundles hanging from the hut's ceiling. He screamed and sobbed until, finally, the sun hoarder gave him one to play with.

Baby-Raven giggled as he rolled the bundle around on the floor, and then, right under the chimney, he let it go. Lights flew upward, out of the house, and spread across the sky as stars.

Baby-Raven began crying again and pointed to the next bundle of light. Again, his grandfather gave it to him to play with, and again baby-Raven "accidentally" released it, and the moon floated up into the sky, too.

Now the sun hoarder was getting concerned. But when baby-Raven started crying again, this time pointing to the secure box where the brightest light was kept, the sun hoarder relented and gave the box to his grandson. Raven opened it up and released the daylight, which flew out and spread over the land. In the confusion Raven turned back into his true form and flew up through the chimney and into the daylight.

## WHY RAVEN DOESN'T BUG OCTOPUS ANYMORE

This story comes from the Nootka people of British Columbia. One day Octopus was walking on a beach, digging for clams with a stick. Raven appeared and asked, "Octopus, are you digging for clams?" Octopus didn't respond, so Raven asked again, "Octopus, are you digging for clams?" And then he asked again, and again. And again. And again.

Suddenly, Octopus grabbed him with her tentacles. "I'm glad you asked that question," she said. "Yes, I am digging for clams. These are clams. And I am digging them." As the tide began to come in, he thanked her and asked her to let him go, but she didn't. She just kept repeating that answer, over and over, until the water rose high enough that Raven drowned.

But it was okay—Raven was immortal, and the next day he was back to life. From then on he didn't ask Octopus any annoying questions.

# SEDNA

## THE SPIRIT OF SEA CREATURES

## SEDNA

**TRADITION:** Inuit

**HOME:** Adlivun, the underworld

**ALSO KNOWN AS:** Nuliayuk, Takanakapsaluk

Not much lives in the Arctic Circle. Chilly summers, frigid winters, and months without sunlight mean that few plants, and even fewer things that eat plants, can survive. Just about all you'll find up there are fish and things that eat fish—seals, walruses, whales, and humans. Little wonder, then, that one of the Arctic's most important deities is a goddess of sea creatures.

Not all people in the Arctic believe in Sedna, and even those who do believe don't necessarily agree on all the details. Here is one common version of the story of Sedna.

## WHY FISH ARE ALL PART SEDNA

A long, long time ago, before Sedna was a goddess, she was just a girl. She lived with her father, Anguta. One day, she met a beautiful seabird, who asked her to sail across the ocean to live with him. She was so dazzled that she packed up her stuff at once and began the long journey to the seabird's home.

But as soon as she came within sight of his nest, she knew she had made a mistake. The place was cold and disgusting (if you've ever seen or smelled a seabird, you will understand). And what's more, there was no food to eat. So, hungry and cold, Sedna called out to her father to rescue her.

SO DREAMY...

CAW!

Sedna had to wait a full year until Anguta arrived in his canoe with dogs and weapons. Once he killed the bird, Sedna boarded his canoe for the long trip home. But soon the seabird's friends caught up to them, and they had revenge on their minds. They used their powers over the winds to create a huge storm.

As the wind blew stronger and stronger and the waves crashed higher and higher, Anguta panicked and threw Sedna overboard. She swam after him, but when she managed to grab hold of the boat, Anguta took out his knife and cut off all her fingers. Sedna sank into the ocean. As the storm raged overhead, her fingers transformed into all the sea creatures that people eat—fish, seals, even whales.

Once the storm had passed, Anguta leaned back in his boat to sleep. But Sedna hadn't stopped swimming. She sneaked back aboard, tied her father up, and fed his hands and feet to his dogs. *That* woke him up.

Anguta yelled and thrashed as he tried to escape, making such a ruckus that he and Sedna were both swallowed by the earth itself. Sedna wound up in Adlivun, the underworld, where she rules to this day.

# SETH

## THE USURPER

# SETH

**TRADITION:** Egyptian
**HOME:** The sky
**ALSO KNOWN AS:** Set, Typhon (Greek)

Seth is the greatest warrior in all of Egyptian mythology: a huge, dumb, savage fighter with just enough ambition to be dangerous. He killed his own brother, Osiris, in order to steal the kingship from him, and then nearly killed Osiris's son, Horus, when he came to reclaim his birthright.

Ultimately, Seth was defeated and forced to give up his ill-gotten throne, in favor of another job more worthy of his talents. Now he protects the solar barque that carries the sun god Ra across the sky, standing on its prow with his spear always ready to repel assaults by Apep, a huge, ancient serpent that devours the world.

Seth is a god of plagues, storms, droughts, invading armies, crime, and more or less everything that made ancient Egyptians' lives more difficult. There were temples dedicated to earning his favor and temples dedicated to banishing him by destroying sources of his power. He might be more trouble than he's worth, but if there is a hostile army banging at your gates, a little Seth goes a long way.

Priests of Horus at Edfu hated Seth so much that they had a whole day dedicated to destroying him. The ritual involved dismembering a "wild ass," which might also be a fair name for Seth himself.

## THE SETH ANIMAL

Seth has the head and tail of a mythological creature that scholars call the "Seth animal." It's a long, lean, black thing, with square ears, a forked tail, and a downturned snout—like a mean dog crossed with an even meaner aardvark. Interestingly, some say that something like the Seth animal might have actually existed once but has since gone extinct.

# How We Know What We Know About Egyptian Mythology

Egyptologists (folks who study ancient Egypt) have it relatively easy, mythologically speaking, because Egyptians left them with a lot to work with. They had a written language and a hot, dry climate that is great for preserving things. The knowledge of their language was eventually lost, but the 1799 discovery of the Rosetta stone, a hunk of rock with the same words written in Egyptian (which we didn't know) and Greek (which we did), has allowed scholars to begin translating sources on ancient Egyptian mythology, including:

- **Tombs:** The Egyptians believed that, after death, the spirits of the dead had to journey through the underworld, and they packed their tombs with things that might help on the journey. These included spells, myths, and instructions painted on tomb walls.

- **Monuments:** You would be hard pressed to find ancient monuments with more text on them than Egyptian ones. Obelisks, stelae, statues, and sacred buildings are covered in useful information.

- **Temple libraries:** By searching the ruins of ancient temples, scholars have recovered parts of still-readable scrolls. Many of them record rituals and hymns that reference myths.

- **Egyptian literature:** In addition to purely religious texts, we have found plenty of other pieces of Egyptian writing over the years. Some of these give us valuable insight into ancient Egyptian culture, which we can then use to make better sense of their mythology.

- **Greek and Roman records:** The kingdoms of Egypt had lots of contact with other cultures in the Mediterranean, including the Greeks and Romans, who did a lot of writing. These sources multiplied once Egypt was conquered by the Greeks and Romans.

# SHIVA

## THE DESTROYER

# SHIVA

**TRADITION:** Indian/Hindu
**HOME:** Mount Kailash
**ALSO KNOWN AS:** Siva

Depending on the story in question, Shiva can vary a lot. He is a god of destruction and a god of life. He rejects worldly pleasures in favor of constant meditation, but he's also a loving, engaged husband. He's a perfectly disciplined master of yoga, but he's also a ferocious god of storms. He's a lord of animals and a lord of ghosts. He's a creator and a protector and, most famously, a destroyer.

Someday Shiva will destroy everything in existence and return it to the formless chaos from which it came. But that won't happen for a long, long time, and even then, he will only destroy an illusion. The truth behind the illusion will continue on through the next world, and the next, and so on forever. (Complicated, huh?) In the meantime, Shiva destroys other things, including demons, illusions, and things that bug him while he meditates.

## SHIVA, DESTROYER OF POISON

In one of the most famous Hindu myths, the gods and their sometimes-enemies, the asuras, joined forces to churn up a whole ocean so they could raise the treasures from its depths. They recovered powerful weapons, mystical creatures, a few goddesses, and a drink that could make anyone immortal. But they also brought up something awful: Halahala, a poison that could kill the universe itself.

Luckily, before it could do any permanent damage, Shiva drank it all. His wife, Parvati, squeezed him by the throat, preventing the poison from reaching his stomach. Shiva's life was saved, but his throat turned permanently blue.

DON'T YOU DIE ON ME.

## The Lord of the Dance

This image is called the Shiva Nataraja, or *Shiva as Lord of the Dance*. It's one of the most common images of Shiva and has existed in one form or another for more than fifteen hundred years. It's also bursting with symbolism, telling you everything you need to know about Shiva.

- Shiva dances within an endless circle of fire, representing time without end.

- In one right hand, he plays the drum and makes the first sounds of creation.

- In one left hand, he holds Agni, the fire that destroys the universe.

- His lower hands are in symbolic poses that calm fear and offer salvation.

- He stands on a squat little jerk who represents Apasmara Purusha, the ignorance that keeps people from enlightenment.

## SHIVA, DESTROYER OF EVERYTHING

While Shiva meditated one day, Parvati sneaked up behind him and playfully covered his eyes. But when Shiva's eyes went dark, so did the whole universe. No one, anywhere, could see anything. Fortunately, Shiva grew a third eye in the middle of his forehead and used it to light everything back up. Unfortunately, it lit everything up with white-hot flames and killed everyone and everything, including Parvati's father. Parvati, horrified at the destruction, begged Shiva to fix it, so he shut his third eye and brought everyone back to life.

PREPARE...TO...LOOOOOOVE

## SHIVA, DESTROYER OF LOVE

The gods were desperate. Their kingdom was under attack by a demon named Tarakasura, who could only be defeated by Shiva's son. The thing was, Shiva didn't have a son. And since he spent all his time meditating and refused all physical pleasure, he wasn't likely to make one. If they were to survive, the gods realized, they had to make Shiva fall in love. They arranged for Shiva's wife, Parvati, to team up with Kama, the god of love.

Parvati stood in front of the meditating Shiva, and Kama shot Shiva with one of his love arrows. Shiva, furious at the interruption, opened his third eye at Kama and turned him instantly to ash. But the arrow did its job: Shiva and Parvati made a son, Kartikeya, who beat Tarakasura handily. Oh, and don't worry about Kama. His body may be gone, but his spirit lives on, spreading love throughout the universe.

## SHIVA, DESTROYER OF COWS

By some accounts, all cows in the world were born from the goddess Kamadhenu, the Mother of All Cows. She gave birth to huge herds of them, all pure and white and full of life-giving milk. But as the cows kept coming, they began causing problems. The world filled up with their milk, and Shiva's mountain home became an island in a creamy white ocean.

The commotion woke Shiva from his meditation, and he opened his third eye, angrily blasting the cows with fire and burning them until their fur turned brown. Hoping to save the remaining cows, the gods offered Shiva the world's best bull, Nandi. Shiva took it as his mount and allowed the cows (or what was left of them) to survive.

# SUN WUKONG

## THE MONKEY KING

# SUN WUKONG

**TRADITION:** Chinese
**ALSO KNOWN AS:** The Monkey King

un Wukong wasn't always the Monkey King. He was born a normal, mortal monkey and would have died long ago if he hadn't stolen immortality from the gods. He's a master of martial arts and magical transformations, taking forms ranging from tiny bugs to massive giants. He's cheeky and arrogant and not especially wise, but he's also cunning and strong enough to defeat more or less every single member of the Celestial Bureaucracy of Chinese gods.

Sun Wukong (pronounced "sun woo-kong") has appeared in myths since at least the Song dynasty (960–1279 CE), but he is best known for his starring role in a sixteenth-century novel called *Journey to the West*. It tells the story of Xuanzang, a legendary monk who traveled to India to translate the sacred books of Buddhism into Chinese. Since then, it's been adapted into books, movies, and even an opera. Here is a summary of Sun Wukong's part of the story.

## THE STORY OF SUN WUKONG

Long before he was the Monkey King, and even before he was a monkey, Sun Wukong was a stone egg. He wasn't inside an egg—he *was* an egg. And that egg transformed itself into a monkey.

Even in his youth Sun Wukong displayed the cunning, ambition, and lawlessness that would come to define him. He rose to become the king of the monkeys and lived a life of ease and pleasure. But that all changed the day he saw an old monkey die and realized that someday he would die, too. Sun Wukong didn't want to die, so he left his island kingdom in search of immortality.

His travels brought him to a mountain monastery where a great Taoist priest accepted him as a student. Sun Wukong was a quick study, and he soon mastered numerous martial arts, magical transformations, and even the skill of cloud-dancing (jumping really, really, really far). The only things he failed to learn were wisdom and humility. All his new power went right to his head, so he was expelled for being an arrogant, cheeky show-off.

Sun Wukong returned home and spent his time finding demons, beating them up, and taking their stuff. In the process, he acquired what became his signature weapon, the Ruyi Jingu Bang, a magical, six-ton metal staff that could change size. He shrank it to the length of a toothpick and stored it behind his ear.

Sun Wukong spent years collecting ever more riches and power, but he still wasn't immortal. Shortly before he was destined to die, Sun Wukong found his way to the Registers of Death, the books in which everyone's births and deaths were recorded. He flipped through the pages, erasing his name and those of all the other monkeys he could find. And that's how he finally came to the attention of the Jade Emperor, leader of the gods.

The Jade Emperor could see the threat Sun Wukong posed and decided to keep a close watch on him. He appointed him stable boy to the gods, which made Sun Wukong really happy until he realized that being a horse janitor wasn't the honor the gods had made it out to be.

Outraged, Sun Wukong released the horses and returned to his island. The gods sent armies to punish him, but he defeated them all. Eventually the Jade Emperor offered a truce, and a position worthy of the Monkey King: guardian of the grove where the gods grew their immortality-granting peaches.

Again Sun Wukong accepted, and again he did his job. But one day, he found out that all the other gods had gone to a huge

...AND HERE IS YOUR HONORABLE SCEPTER OF OFFICE.

ooooOOooooo...

Sun Wukong may be strong, but he has never been able to sit still long enough to meditate.

banquet without him. So he quit—but not before gobbling up some immortality peaches. This time, the gods caught him. They stuck him in a cauldron for weeks to boil out the immortality, but something must have gone wrong, because he popped out stronger than ever, with glowing, diamond-hard eyes and a hankering for revenge.

Finally, the Jade Emperor sought the help of the only other being he was sure could overpower the Monkey King: the Buddha himself. The Buddha trapped Sun Wukong under his hand (which was also a mountain) for five hundred years. When the gods finally released Sun Wukong, they put a metal band around his head to keep him in line. If he ever misbehaved again, someone would say the magic phrase, and the band would tighten until his head was crushed.

# SUSANOO

## THE SHORT-TEMPERED STORM GOD

## SUSANOO

**TRADITION:** Japanese/Shinto
**HOME:** Yomi (the underworld)
**ALSO KNOWN AS:** Susanoo-no-Mikoto

Susanoo (pronounced "su-san-o-wo") is not a nice god. When he's angry, he destroys stuff. When he's bored, he destroys stuff. When he's happy, he celebrates by destroying stuff. He has caused natural disasters just by walking from place to place, and he throws tantrums so awful that the other gods kicked him out of heaven. It's not that he's evil, although he can be cruel. It's just that he's big, brash, uncontrolled, and powerful enough that you can measure his moods on the Richter scale.

## SUSANOO IS MEAN TO HIS DAD

When Susanoo was born from his father Izanagi's nose, his father divided the universe between Susanoo and his siblings. To Susanoo's sister, the sun goddess Amaterasu, Izanagi granted the sky and the Celestial Plains, home of the gods. To Susanoo's brother, the moon god Tsuki-yomi, Izanagi assigned the night sky. And to Susanoo, he gave the ocean. While Amaterasu and Tsuki-yomi graciously accepted their new roles, Susanoo threw a tantrum. He didn't want some stupid ocean! He wanted to live with his mother, Izanami, in the underworld. Izanagi angrily granted his request.

## SUSANOO IS MEAN TO HIS SISTER

Before leaving for the underworld, Susanoo rampaged up to Amaterasu's home in heaven to say goodbye.

When Amaterasu saw him charging toward her, disasters and mayhem in his wake, she suspected the worst and prepared herself. When Susanoo arrived to find her armed with a bow and ready for battle, he claimed that he meant no harm and offered to prove it with a competition: Whichever of them could create more gods would win and be proven right.

Amaterasu took his sword, broke it into three pieces, chewed them up, and spat out three new goddesses. When it was Susanoo's turn, he took some of Amaterasu's hair beads, chewed them up, spat out five gods, and declared himself the winner.

Amaterasu disagreed. Since they came from her hair beads, she reasoned, they were her gods. But that didn't stop Susanoo. He celebrated his alleged victory by ruining the gods' rice fields and irrigation ditches, pooping in the dining hall, and throwing a pony through the roof of Amaterasu's weaving room, killing a goddess in the process.

The whole ordeal left Amaterasu so shaken that she went into hiding, and it took eight hundred gods working together to get her out. Once she was back, those eight hundred gods turned their attention to punishing Susanoo. They sentenced him to a painful makeover: They shaved his beard, cut off his toenails and fingernails, and forced him through several more embarrassing rituals before kicking him out of the heavens permanently.

## SUSANOO IS MEAN TO A DRAGON

Even after two banishments, Susanoo didn't go straight to the underworld. First he wandered around the earth for a while, having adventures in ancient Japan. The most famous of these began when he ran into an old couple and a beautiful girl, all crying. They told him they were a family—or what was left of it, anyway. An eight-headed and eight-tailed dragon named Yamota-no-orochi had eaten seven of the couple's daughters and would be back soon to eat the youngest, Kusa-nada-hime. Susanoo revealed that he was a god and offered his help, on one condition: Once he dealt with the dragon, he got to marry Kusa-nada-hime. They agreed.

Inside one of the dragon's tails Susanoo found the legendary sword Kusanagi-no-Tsurugi (*Grass-Cutting Sword*). He eventually passed it on to Amaterasu, who gave it to the first emperor of Japan. Officially, it's presented to each new emperor at his coronation—but except for emperors and a few priests, no one has actually seen it in centuries.

First, Susanoo turned the girl into a comb and stuck her in his hair for safekeeping. Then he had her parents fill eight tubs with rice wine and place them on eight platforms, surrounded by a fence with eight holes. Once it was ready, they left, and Susanoo hid and waited.

When the dragon finally arrived and found the wine, it stuck its heads through the holes to drink. Susanoo waited until it was good and drunk and then leaped into action, slicing and cutting the dragon until nothing was left but tiny pieces. He then changed Kusa-nada-hime back into a human, and they were married.

# TANE

### THE LORD OF THE FOREST

# TANE

**TRADITION:** Maori
**ALSO KNOWN AS:** Tane Mahuta

The Maori of New Zealand have one of the best-documented mythologies in all of Oceania and the Pacific. Their most important god, Tane, is a god of birds, wood, and forests, the creator of humanity, and the reason that there is space between the earth and the sky. His forests provide food and wood, and his gifts and inventions have made the Polynesians some of history's greatest mariners, allowing them to explore and settle thousands of miles of islands and archipelagoes using nothing but wood canoes.

## THE SEPARATION OF THE WORLD

In the beginning, there was nothing. No darkness, no watery void—nothing. And then there was Io, a vague, dark creator god. From Io came a god and a goddess: Rangi, the sky, and Papa, the earth. While they were technically separate, they held on to each other so tightly that they looked like a seashell. Together, without once loosening their grip, they had six kids: Tane, god of forests and birds; Tangaroa, god of the sea; Tu, god of war; Rongo, god of farmable plants; Haumia, god of wild plants; and Tawhiri, god of wind and storms.

From birth, each child was squished between their parents. Things were pretty cramped. But it got even worse after Papa moved her arm enough that, just for a second, all six kids could see daylight. After that, they wanted more.

One by one, each god tried and failed to push their parents apart. Then Tu came up with a new plan that proved effective, if violent: He cut off Rangi's arms. The gods had no trouble separating Rangi and Papa then, and Tane kept them apart with wooden poles. Ever since, Rangi and Papa have cried for each other. Rangi's tears became the rain, and Papa's, the morning mist.

But Tawhiri, who hadn't wanted his parents violently separated, sent winds and hurricanes against the other gods. His winds snapped Tane's trees to pieces and sent Tangaroa's oceans crashing and churning. Tangaroa's children fled in opposite directions. One, the ancestor of fish, hid under the ocean. The other, ancestor of reptiles, hid in Tane's forests. Tangaroa blamed Tane for keeping his reptile kid from him, and the two have been at war ever since. Tangaroa causes floods and tidal waves, and Tane teaches people to make boats to conquer the sea.

There is a huge tree in New Zealand that locals named Tane Mahuta after the god. No one is sure how old it is, but estimates range from twelve hundred to two thousand years!

## TANE'S DAUGHTER, DEATH

Tane had a lot of offspring, including all sorts of animals and plants and even rocks. One day, his father, Rangi, suggested that Tane make a woman so he could have human babies. So he created Hine-titama, the first human.

For a while it worked out exactly like Tane had hoped. But when Hine-titama realized that the guy she was making babies with was her father, she ran away. She didn't stop until she reached the underworld, where she became Hine-nui-te-po, goddess of the underworld and death. Her revenge was simple and permanent: Everyone and everything that Tane ever made will one day die. Tane has made new people since, but eventually every one of them has died.

## TANE AND THE BASKETS OF KNOWLEDGE

A long time ago, all important knowledge was kept in three baskets: one with knowledge of love, one with knowledge of religion, and one with knowledge of survival and war. But knowledge does no good stuck in baskets, so Io gave the knowledge to Tane with orders to spread it throughout the world. Tane traveled to all the islands of Polynesia, building temples and leaving the knowledge inside them.

A horrible god named Whiro sent hordes of creepy-crawly bugs to stop him, but it didn't work—Tane found Whiro and kicked his butt all the way down to the underworld. Whiro's bugs remained on Earth, though, and their descendants are still with us as spiders, moths, and ants.

EW EW
EW EW
EW...

CRUNCH

# TENGRI

**THE ETERNAL SKY**

# TENGRI

**TRADITION:** Central Asian/Turkic
**HOME:** The Heavens

Most of central Asia is a long, flat, grassy plain called the Great Steppe. For thousands of years, it was home to nomadic, horse-riding civilizations, who followed their herds from place to place and raided one another and whatever settled people lived nearby. Sometimes, a whole bunch of them would unite under a single leader (for instance, Atilla the Hun or Genghis Khan) and conquer the known world. For most of their history, despite frequent contact with other cultures, the peoples of the steppe held one god above all others: Tengri.

No one is sure what Tengri looks like. As far as his worshippers are concerned, that's beside the point. His name means "sky" and that's what he is: vast, formless, infinite, and eternal.

The earth goddess may have made people's bodies, but Tengri gave them souls, and Tengri alone decided when they died. He also decided when civilizations ended, or at least which rulers got to rule. And if a leader ever lost power—if, say, he was conquered or kicked out or the tribes who followed him decided to follow someone else—it was because Tengri had judged him unworthy. There's a reason Genghis Khan started all his declarations with "By the will of Eternal Blue Heaven": Without Tengri, Khan was just some guy on a horse.

LOOKS LIKE TENGRI CHOSE SOMEONE ELSE.

HURK

Nowadays, most of the people living on the steppe are Muslim or Buddhist. But Tengri survives in the modern Turkish word for god: *tanrı*.

## THE GREAT ETERNAL CREATOR-GOOSE

This is just one of many central Asian creation stories.

In the beginning there was endless water, and flying above it was a pure white goose. That goose was Tengri. After an eternity, Tengri heard a voice from below, calling out to him to create. So Tengri created Er Kishi, a darker, meaner god, who joined him above the water.

They flew together, until Er Kishi got arrogant and tried to fly higher than Tengri. As a result, Er Kishi lost his ability to fly at all. As he tumbled, flightless, into the water, he called for Tengri to save him. Tengri raised a hill of earth from the water, and on that hill grew the Cosmic Tree, and from that tree grew the rest of the gods.

Some accounts say Tengri later married the spirit of the earth, and together they created people. She produced the bodies, and he provided the souls. Tengri flew back up to the heavens, but he still helps the people of Earth.

Er Kishi, on the other hand, stuck around Earth and does his best to lead people astray.

DON'T DO IT, ER KISHI!

I'M DOING IT!

# TEZCATLIPOCA

## THE LORD OF THE SMOKING MIRROR

# TEZCATLIPOCA

**TRADITION:** Mesoamerican
**ALSO KNOWN AS:** Black Tezcatlipoca

A powerful and sometimes sinister god haunted the Mesoamerican world. He had many names. Some called him Yaotl, "enemy." Some called him "the Left-Handed One." (Medieval Mesoamericans considered left-handedness a sign of evil.) But most called him Tezcatlipoca (pronouced "tez-cat-leap-*oh*-cah"), "the Smoking Mirror."

He is a god of weapons, battles, illness, and discord, often depicted in opposition to his nicer brother, Quetzalcoatl. He is the night sun, the dark sun, the sun as it passes through the underworld. He is a complex god, a patron of warriors and kings, but also of thieves and foul magic. His magical obsidian mirror can show the future and see into people's hearts.

But while he might be dangerous and deceitful and bring ruin to people and the worlds they live in, Tezcatlipoca isn't all bad. You probably wouldn't want to draw his attention, but he can be useful in the right circumstances. According to one myth, when the Aztecs were searching for a homeland, it was Tezcatlipoca who guided them with visions from his mirror. And while the wars he caused were awful, they were also the main way that the Aztecs captured prisoners to sacrifice—the Aztecs believed that if they ran out of people to sacrifice to the sun god, the world would end.

## HOW TEZCATLIPOCA INVENTED DOGS

One old couple survived the flood that destroyed the fourth world by floating on a boat. When they finally found some land to camp on, they made a fire and cooked some fish for dinner. But the smoke from their fire floated up and annoyed the gods, who complained to Tezcatlipoca. He came down to the old couple, cut off their heads, and attached them to their backsides, and thus created the first dogs.

WOOF?

WOOF.

## Five Worlds, Four (and Counting) Apocalypses

Many Mesoamerican peoples believed that there were other worlds before ours, destroyed in ancient disasters caused by the gods. The Aztec creation myth lists five worlds:

### THE FIRST WORLD

**Ruler:** Tezcatlipoca

**People:** A race of giants so strong they could pull up trees with their bare hands

**How it ended:** Quetzalcoatl knocked Tezcatlipoca into the ocean. Tezcatlipoca returned as an enormous jaguar, and then other jaguars ate all the giants.

### THE SECOND WORLD

**Ruler:** Quetzalcoatl, god of wind

**People:** Gatherers who ate mesquite tree seeds

**How it ended:** Tezcatlipoca carried Quetzalcoatl and all the people on Earth away in a huge hurricane. The surviving people became monkeys.

### THE THIRD WORLD

**Ruler:** Tlaloc, god of rain

**People:** Farmers who ate primitive grain

**How it ended:** Quetzalcoatl burned up the world in a rain of fire and ash. The survivors became butterflies, dogs, and turkeys.

### THE FOURTH WORLD

**Ruler:** Chalchiuhtlicue, goddess of rivers, lakes, and oceans

**People:** Folks who ate a seed called acicintli

**How it ended:** A huge flood washed everything away, including the mountains that held up the sky. The survivors became fish.

### THE FIFTH WORLD

**Ruler:** Fire god Tonatiuh, or war god Huitzilopochtli, depending on who you ask

**People:** Us

**How it will end:** If the gods ever stop receiving human sacrifices, Tezcatlipoca will steal the sun, and the world will be destroyed.

Tezcatlipoca isn't the only Tezcatlipoca. To be specific, he's the Black Tezcatlipoca, as opposed to his brothers, the White Tezcatlipoca (aka Quetzalcoatl), the Blue Tezcatlipoca (aka Huitzilopochtli, god of war), and the Red Tezcatlipoca (aka Xipe Totec, god of farming).

## TEZCATLIPOCA, QUETZALCOATL, AND THE GIANT WITH A BUNCH OF MOUTHS

After the fourth world was washed away, and in spite of the fact that they had both destroyed worlds in the past, Tezcatlipoca and Quetzalcoatl teamed up to create a new, fifth world. In one version of the myth, they raised the fallen sky and turned into trees to hold it aloft—one tree covered with dark mirrors, the other with green feathers. By way of thanks, they were made lords of the heavens and stars.

In another version, they made the new world safe by killing a monster named Tlaltecuhtli. She was a huge giant with gnashing mouths on every joint, all hungry for flesh. Tezcatlipoca and Quetzalcoatl turned into giant serpents and ambushed her, wrapping themselves around her arms and legs and tearing her in half. They threw her bottom half upward, and it became the heavens. But they didn't throw her top half, and it became the earth. Her hair became the trees, flowers, and herbs, her skin became the grasses, her nose became mountains, her eyes small caves and water sources, and her mouth giant caves and rivers.

# THOR

## HAMMER-SMASHING GOD OF THUNDER

## THOR

**TRADITION:** Norse

**HOME:** Asgard

**ALSO KNOWN AS:** Thunor (Old English), Donar (German)

There aren't many gods more famous than Thor. It might be because he's cool-looking, or because he stars in a lot of good stories. It might be that he happened to be really popular right when most of what we know about Norse paganism was written down. It might also be the world-famous comic book character he inspired.

But for all people think they know about Thor, there is a lot they get wrong. He isn't blond, for one thing—his beard has always been red. He isn't related to the trickster god Loki. He has never worn a horned helmet (which are far more common in modern Viking costumes than they ever were in Viking times). And his home in Asgard is a traditional Viking longhouse, not a rainbow space station like in that one movie.

The real Thor is a god of thunder and storms, and a patron of warriors, soldiers, and the people they defend. He roars through the sky on a great, thundering chariot and throws his hammer, Mjollnir, with the power and speed of lightning. He is big, burly, short-tempered, and not especially bright. He doesn't scheme like his father, Odin, or play tricks like Loki. When he has a problem, he hits it. When the problem survives, he hits it some more. Most of Thor's stories end with a flattened, dead giant on the end of Thor's hammer, and that's the way he likes it. But for variety's sake, here are a few more interesting stories.

## THOR VS. THE OCEAN

The Norse gods love to drink—one of their most valuable possessions is the Mead of Poetry—but even among gods, Thor is an especially skilled drinker. Once, a giant goaded Thor into entering a drinking competition. What Thor didn't know was that the giant had connected the bottom of his drinking horn to the ocean itself. Thor drank, and drank, and drank, until his stomach bulged and he teetered over, defeated. He couldn't drink the whole ocean, but the giant was impressed all the same. By the time Thor collapsed, he had created a whole new shoreline.

When Christians in Scandinavia began wearing necklaces with crosses, Norse pagans started wearing their own necklaces with hammers of Thor. Silversmiths were happy to sell both.

## THOR VS. A CAT

Next, the giant challenged Thor to a test of strength and brought in a cat for Thor to lift. Thor bent down and tried to pick it up, but the cat wouldn't budge. He tried again, wrapping his arms around it and heaving with all his might, but he barely managed to get one of its paws off the ground. In the end, Thor had to admit defeat. It was only later that the giant revealed his trick: The "cat" wasn't a cat at all, but a magical disguise. Thor had actually been trying to lift Jörmungandr, a snake so large that it encircled the whole world.

## THOR VS. AN OLD WOMAN

After the cat incident, Thor was fed up and dared anyone to wrestle him. The giant claimed a weakling like Thor wasn't worth his time and offered in his place a frail old woman. The match commenced, but the little old lady proved more resilient than she looked. Try as he might, Thor couldn't throw her. Then the woman grabbed Thor. As the minutes passed and the woman bore down on him, Thor began to wobble, shakily dropping to one knee before the giant called off the match. The giant then explained his trick: Thor hadn't fought an old woman. He had fought old age itself.

## THOR VS. MARRIAGE

One morning Thor awoke to find that his hammer, Mjollnir, was missing. This was *bad*—Mjollnir was the most powerful weapon the gods of Asgard had against giants, and without it they were defenseless. The gods fanned out to search for the hammer, and sent Loki in the form of a falcon to search from the air.

Panic had turned to quiet dread by the time Loki returned. He announced that he had found the hammer—sort of. It had been stolen by Thrym, king of the giants, and buried deep underground. Thrym would only return it if Freya, goddess of beauty, married him.

Freya refused, of course. But the watchman god Heimdall suggested an alternative: Thor would put on a dress and veil and go in Freya's place. And since Thor wasn't the best actor, Loki would go with him, disguised as "Freya's" maidservant. Thor grumbled, but without any better ideas, he was forced to agree.

They arrived at Thrym's fortress to find a great feast waiting for them. Thor dove in and ate the whole thing: an ox, eight salmon, tons of mead, and countless side dishes. When Thrym commented that he had never seen a woman eat so much, Loki explained that poor Freya was so in love with him that she hadn't been able to eat for a week. Thrym excitedly pulled back Freya's veil to kiss her but jumped back when he saw Thor's rage-filled eyes. But before he could react, Loki jumped in again, reassuring him that Freya's eyes were merely tired from a week of sleepless, lovesick nights.

After the meal, the wedding commenced. Thrym and "Freya" sat together, and when it was time, Thrym revealed Mjollnir. As a show of good faith, he put it on his new bride's lap. Thor grabbed it, swung it, and smashed him dead. Then he smashed the rest of the giants in attendance and stomped his way back home.

"WEAR A DRESS, THOR."
"YOU'RE SO PRETTY, THOR."
I'LL SHOW THEM PRETTY.
GRUMBLE GRUMBLE GRUMBLE...

# THOTH

## THE LUNAR SCRIBE

# THOTH

**TRADITION**: Egyptian
**HOME**: Duat
**ALSO KNOWN AS**: Djehuti

For most of human history, there was no such thing as writing. It's one of the main reasons studying mythology can be so challenging—can you imagine how many stories we would still have if folks had known how to write them down? Even in places that did have writing, like Egypt, very few people knew how to write.

Writing was a source of power. With a paintbrush and the right training, a person could transform ink into a permanent source of knowledge. To your average ancient Egyptian, it must have seemed like magic.

Thoth is the inventor of writing and god of everything it represented in Egypt: knowledge, wisdom, secrets, and magic. He is a moon god, and since the Egyptians told time using the phases of the moon, he is also a god of time and calendars. He is the note taker and bookkeeper of the gods, recording everything that happens each day and organizing it into a report for Ra, the sun god, each morning.

All knowledge originates with Thoth. He knows the future and the past. Some have even claimed that he recorded all knowledge that humans would ever need in forty-two papyrus scrolls—although if he did, they are long gone. There is a rumor that one copy might have been held at the fabled Library of Alexandria, but the library got burned up, so we don't know for sure.

## THOTH IN THE AFTERLIFE

You might think that Thoth's duties as a moon god would keep him away from the underworld, but Thoth is a frequent presence in the afterlife. As a god of writing and magic, he is directly and indirectly involved with the Books of the Dead, the sacred books of prayers and spells that help the deceased overcome the many dangers of the underworld.

Once they reach the end of their journey, spirits enter the court of the king of the dead, Osiris. But according to some traditions, first they meet Thoth. While they try to convince him to put in a good word for them, he calmly weighs their heart against a feather that represents truth and records the result. Then he passes the information, and the souls, to Osiris for a final judgment.

## JUDGE THOTH PRESIDING

In addition to his job as a scribe, Thoth is often called upon to judge disagreements or negotiate with wayward gods. He is honest and perceptive, and his calm arguments have resolved many disagreements. On the occasions when the disagreement turns violent, he is an extremely skilled healer as well. Here are a few of the cases where Thoth has stepped in:

- When the Eye of Ra (a goddess) abandoned her father and vanished in the desert, it was Thoth who tracked her down and eventually convinced her to return.

- When the goddess Isis collected all the scattered pieces of her dead husband, Osiris, she couldn't bring him back to life on her own, according to some tellings. It was Thoth who taught her the magic she needed.

- When the god Seth was brought to trial for killing his brother, Osiris, Thoth represented the dead god both in and out of the courtroom. He also kept careful watch on Osiris's son, Horus.

- When Horus grew up and challenged Seth for the throne, Thoth helped resolve the conflict.

- When Isis later wound up without a head, and when her son, Horus, had his eye destroyed, Thoth repaired or replaced them both.

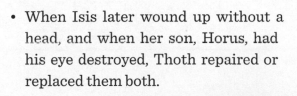

DOES IT... AH... ...FEEL...HEAVY...?

PUMP PUMP PUMP

# UNDERWORLDS

AND OTHER AFTERLIVES

## DIYU

The mythological Chinese afterlife is a mixture of Taoist, Buddhist, Confucian, and traditional folk beliefs. Upon death, all souls are judged by a spiritual magistrate. In extremely rare cases, a worthy spirit is allowed passage to the heavens. Everyone else gets the underground prison of Diyu, where they are put through a well-organized program of torture and misery until they have atoned for their sins, followed by reincarnation on Earth.

MMM NO, THIS IS FORM 43.A. YOU NEED FORM 43.B.

## THE ELYSIAN FIELDS

While most ancient Greeks were destined for Hades, the underworld, a few were rewarded with a trip to the Elysian fields, a bright, happy island paradise. Some sources say that only the greatest heroes went there, while others say that extremely virtuous nonheroes were allowed in, too. Either way, admission was strictly limited.

## THE FIELD OF REEDS

The ancient Egyptian afterlife was a wonderful place—the trick was getting there. First, the dead soul would follow the god Anubis through the underworld to the hall of its king, Osiris, and wait in line to be judged. When its turn came, the soul had to swear it hadn't sinned and present its heart to be weighed against a feather. If the heart was lighter than the feather, the soul was allowed to move on to the Field of Reeds, where it would reunite with everyone and everything it had loved in life. If the heart was too heavy, the soul was destroyed.

## HADES

The Greek underworld of Hades is a dark, damp, moldy place, guarded by a huge three-headed dog and crisscrossed by a set of horrible rivers, including the River Styx (hatred), the River Acheron (woe), and the River Lethe (forgetfulness). Dead souls are ferried across by the grizzled boatman Charon and then left to spend eternity silently drifting. Ruling over it all are the god of the dead, whose name is also Hades, and his sometimes-wife, Persephone.

## HEL

Not to be confused with the Christian hell, Hel is the name of both the Norse underworld and the goddess who rules it. Hel is freezing cold, located deep underground, and guarded by walls and rivers. Not all the Norse dead end up here (some are destined for more desirable afterlives), but most of them do. The goddess Hel is a horrible sight—a normal person from the waist up, but a rotten corpse from the waist down.

## IRKALLA

Irkalla is also called the Land of No Return. It's a dark, dusty, and bleak land, ruled over by Ereshkigal, the Mesopotamian goddess of death. Seven gates guard the entrance, and all who enter must leave something behind at each gate. The spirits of the dead who end up here don't feel pain or pleasure or much of anything at all. They just go about their days eating dust, drinking mud, and drifting aimlessly until the end of time.

HMPH. THIS TASTES LIKE DIRT.

IT IS DIRT.

## MICTLAN

According to the Aztecs, most dead souls made their way to the underworld of Mictlan. There they undertook an arduous, four-year journey through nine layers of the underworld. When they finally reached the end, they disappeared forever.

COME ALONG, EVERYONE. LEVEL 9, RIGHT THIS WAY...

## THE OTHERWORLD

The Celts didn't have an underworld, exactly. But they did have an Otherworld, a magical world that exists alongside ours and is home to gods, fairies, monsters, and spirits of the dead. It's a bright, lively place, but not without its dangers, especially for those living mortals who find their way in. During the Festival of Samhain, traditionally celebrated on October 31, the souls of the dead were believed to come back to our world and take revenge on the living. You might recognize that date: We call it Halloween.

## VALHALLA

Upon death, the greatest Viking warriors were believed to be carried from the battlefield by Valkyries, the beautiful female spirits who serve the god Odin. They were brought to the great hall of Valhalla, a huge building made of spears and shields and guarded by wolves and eagles. In Valhalla, they live an ideal afterlife: countless days of fighting and nights of feasting, all in the company of the world's best warriors. Their fighting has a purpose, though. When it's time for Ragnarok, the battle at the end of the world, they will all fight and die alongside Odin—this time, for good.

## XIBALBA

Far to the west, the Maya believed, lies Xibalba, the place of fear. Xibalba is a twisted reflection of our own world, just as vast but far more dangerous. The souls of the dead who journey through Xibalba must contend with rivers of blood, mountains of bone, horrible monsters, and devious traps. Their only hope of escape is to outwit the ruling gods, the lords of the underworld.

## YOMI-NO-KUNI

After her death, the Japanese goddess Izanami descended to rule Yomi-no-kuni, the Shinto underworld. It's a dark, rotten place, deep underground, and its pollution has a way of sticking to you. Its entrance in Japan was sealed by a boulder by Izanami's husband, Izanagi. Given all the awful things inside, that's probably for the best.

DANGER
DO NOT
UNPLUG

# VIRACOCHA

## THE WANDERING CREATOR

# VIRACOCHA

**TRADITION:** Incan/Andean
**HOME:** Somewhere across the ocean
**ALSO KNOWN AS:** Huiracocha, Wiraqoca

The creator god of the Inca empire is a being of great wisdom and power. Unfortunately, we don't know much about him, and even less about other Inca gods. Further complicating things, we have evidence of several different versions of Viracocha, and it's hard to say whether these were the same god, or aspects of the same god, or originally separate gods that the Inca merged into one. However, we do know a bit about how Viracocha created the world.

## VIRACOCHA CREATES THE WORLD

Like many creator gods, Viracocha emerged into wet, empty darkness. His first act was to create the first race of humanity, massive stone giants who lived in the dark. But the giants angered him, so he drowned them all in a flood. According to legend, some of their bodies still exist in the form of the great stone statues at Tiahuanaco in Bolivia.

Having washed away his first attempt, Viracocha tried again. First, he called the sun, moon, and stars out from an island on Lake Titicaca. Then he took some soft stone from the lake's shores and molded it into the first people. He made men, women, and children and painted sets of clothes onto each to show which belonged to which nation. Finally, he gave each nation a language, songs, foods, skills, and everything else they needed to become real civilizations.

Once he was done, Viracocha headed northwest toward the Pacific Ocean, calling forth plants and animals along the way and granting them names and identities. He kept walking when he reached the ocean and disappeared over the horizon, never to be heard from again.

## VIRACOCHA'S SON SEARCH

Another version of Viracocha's naming of the animals gives him a little more character.

While wandering one day, Viracocha ran into a beautiful female huaca named Cavillaca. He fell in love instantly and secretly impregnated her by tampering with a fruit she was eating.

GO ON. WHO'S YOUR FATHER?

## How We Know What We Know About Incan Mythology

The main challenge in learning about Incan mythology is that Spanish colonists destroyed so much of it. Countless golden religious artifacts were melted down into bars and sent back to Spain, and countless religious writings were destroyed and replaced with Bibles. But we can still piece together some of the Incan myths using what sources we do have, including:

- **Spanish accounts:** At various points during and after their conquest, Spanish people asked Andean people about their myths and wrote some of them down. In some cases, this was driven by curiosity or even sympathy. In others, it was colonial authorities trying to learn how they might strengthen their rule or convert more people to Christianity.

- **Native accounts:** We don't have any native sources written before the conquest, but we do have some from after it. But these aren't perfect—a lot of knowledge was already lost.

- **Ruins, temples, and statues:** Stone buildings last a long time, and even if they are toppled, we can learn something by comparing their structures, layouts, and decorations to other things we know.

- **Burials and mummies:** Egyptian mummies might be the most famous in the world, but they are far from the only ones. Many ancient Andean people mummified their dead and stored them in sacred sites, along with important items. These burials give us a lot of hints about what the Incans believed.

- **Modern folk beliefs:** The Spanish may have conquered the Inca state, but they never converted all the people. Even today there are groups living in the mountains and forests and countryside who retain some of the old customs. A lot has changed over the intervening five hundred years, but scholars can gather important hints from those beliefs that have been passed down.

## Huaca What?

*Huaca* is the word for a sacred place in Incan mythology and for the spirit of that place. The Andean landscape is full of them: ponds, lakes, streams, plains, hills, caves, mountains, and monuments, each with its own spirit. Many native Andean families, tribes, and nations believed they descended from the people who emerged from specific huacas in ancient times.

Huacas served as centers for rituals and festivals, destinations for pilgrimages, and tombs for ancestral mummies.

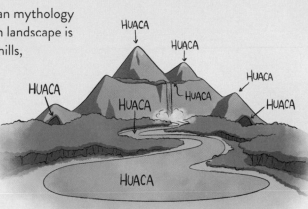

Cavillaca later gave birth to a baby boy. When her child was a year old, she gathered all the gods together and demanded to know who the father was. But they all thought she was gorgeous, and all wanted to marry her, so each claimed he was the father.

The huaca arranged a test. She lined up the gods, placed her child on the ground, and told him to crawl to his father. He crawled and crawled, past dozens of powerful gods in fine clothing, until he reached rag-covered Viracocha and climbed up into his lap.

Cavillaca was furious—dirty old Viracocha?!—and she took her child far away to a distant seashore, where she turned herself and her child to stone.

Viracocha chased after them, asking every creature he passed if they had seen Cavillaca or her son and rewarding or punishing them based on their answer. When he asked the condor, it said he was hot on their trail, so he granted it a long life and plenty of food. When he asked the skunk, it said they were far away, so he cursed it to always smell gross. As he searched, he gave names and traits to all the animals. But he never found Cavillaca or her son.

# VISHNU

## THE PRESERVER

# VISHNU

**TRADITION:** Indian/Hindu
**HOME:** Vai Kuntha
**ALSO KNOW AS:** Visnu

Vishnu isn't just the most important god in the universe. Depending who you ask, he *is* the universe. Brahma creates it and Shiva destroys it, but Vishnu is the one who preserves it and keeps everything working as it should. Usually, this is in an impersonal sense, and while he can be everywhere at once, Vishnu is often more of a concept than a person. But occasionally, when a real threat comes along, Vishnu makes it personal—literally, by incarnating himself as a person or animal and defeating it.

Vishnu wasn't mentioned all that much in the earliest Hindu texts, but his reputation has only grown in the centuries since. He absorbed the roles of some gods, replaced others outright, and adopted still others as avatars, or incarnations.

## VISHNU'S AVATARS

Vishnu can take the form of other things, and most of his stories are about those incarnations, also called avatars. Most sources list ten avatars as the most important, though they don't all agree on which ten. Here is one common list:

**MATSYA:** A fish-man who saved humanity from a huge flood. He warned Manu, the first man, to build a boat and get his family, some sages, and some animals and plant seeds aboard. When the flood came, Matsya dragged the boat to safety at the top of the Himalayas.

**KURMA:** One of the most important Hindu myths is the Churning of the Ocean of Milk, in which the gods and demons stirred up a primordial ocean to dredge treasures from its depths. Before they began, Vishnu transformed into a tortoise and swam to the bottom of the Ocean of Milk. The other gods rested a mountain atop the tortoise so that they could stand on it as they stirred. The plan worked, and the gods retrieved a drink of immortality, a couple of goddesses, and the moon.

**VARAHA:** A boar who saved the world. A demon named Hiranyaksha became immune to a whole bunch of things—including gods, people, and every animal he could think of. Then he stole the earth and hid it under a great ocean. Unfortunately for him, he forgot about boars, so that's what Vishnu turned into to kill him and rescue the earth.

> HMM...TIGERS, BIRDS, MONKEYS, PEOPLE, GODS, TREES, GOATS, BEARS... I HOPE I DIDN'T FORGET ANYTHING...

**NARASIMHA:** A half man, half lion who saved the world from Hiranyaksha's brother, Hiranyakashipu. Hiranyakashipu had arranged it so that he couldn't be killed by gods, people, or animals, at day or night, inside or outside. So Vishnu turned into a man-lion (neither human nor animal) and killed him at dusk (neither day nor night) in a temple doorway (neither inside nor outside).

**VAMANA:** A dwarf who saved the gods from a king named Bali, an asura whose benevolent and just rule allowed him to displace Indra as ruler of the heavens. One day, Vamana showed up at Bali's court and asked for as much land as he could cover in three steps. Bali graciously agreed. But then Vamana started growing and growing and growing, and Bali saw his mistake. In three steps, Vamana crossed all of the earth and the heavens. But he left the underworld to Bali, as thanks for his gift.

**PARASHURAMA:** A man who helped the Brahmins (priests) win a conflict against the Kshatriyas (warriors and rulers).

**RAMA:** The hero of the Ramayana, who destroyed the demon king Ravana.

**KRISHNA:** A popular god in his own right, and one of the main characters in the *Mahabharata*, one of the greatest Hindu epics. There are tons of stories of Krishna's years as a playful, superpowered child, including one in which he uses an entire mountain as an umbrella to protect his neighbors from rain. And there are many more tales about his battles as an adult against his uncle, the evil king Kamsa. But his most famous role was driving the war chariot of Prince Arjuna, which was when he laid out much of the core philosophy of Hinduism.

## How Vishnu Created the Creator of the Universe

Vishnu is the top god of one of the largest branches of Hinduism, Vaishnavism. In the Vaishnavism creation story, Vishnu existed before anything—even Brahma, the so-called Creator. First, Vishnu created an ocean of primordial waters and a hundred-headed serpent to rest on. Then he closed his eyes and meditated. As he did, his creative energy emerged from his belly button in the shape of a lotus flower, and from the lotus's petals emerged Brahma, the Creator, and from Brahma emerged everything else.

**THE BUDDHA:** As more and more people converted to Buddhism in India, some Hindu texts started calling the Buddha an incarnation of Vishnu. This might have been meant as an insult ("your god is just our god in disguise") or it might have been an attempt to reabsorb Buddhism in the way many other gods had already been adopted into Hinduism.

**KALKI:** Vishnu, with a burning sword, riding a white horse. It's probably for the best that the Kalki hasn't actually arrived yet, because whenever he does, our age is over and the world will end.

# THE WAWILAK SISTERS

## WALKERS OF THE DREAMTIME

## THE WAWILAK SISTERS

**TRADITION:** Australian
**HOME:** The Dreamtime
**ALSO KNOWN AS:** Wagilag Sisters, Wagilak Sisters

The native myths of Australia take place in the Dreamtime, the moment when the world came into being, when powerful creatures and spirits roamed the new earth and carved it into its present shape.

These stories are still visible in the hills, mountains, rivers, and lakes where the characters of myth traveled and moved. Even today, you can retrace their paths through the Australian wilderness and access the Dreamtime—if you know the way.

Most of the Aboriginals' myths are kept secret from outsiders. But we do know some of them, including the story of the Wawilak Sisters and their encounter with the Rainbow Snake.

## THE WAWILAK SISTERS AND THE RAINBOW SNAKE

Two sisters emerged from the ocean, walking from the waves onto the sandy shore. The older sister had a baby in her arms, and the younger one was pregnant and due to give birth soon. They headed north into the interior of the continent, feeding themselves with foraged plants and animals they hunted with their spears. As they went, they named all the plants and animals they found.

After a long walk, they came to the Mirarrmina watering hole. As they stopped to rest, the younger sister felt her first contractions. The baby was coming. The older sister made her a bed and went out to hunt. She returned with an animal, but when she prepared a fire and tried to cook it, it leaped back to life and escaped into the watering hole. Again the older sister hunted an animal, and again she tried to cook it, and again it came back to life and escaped.

She kept trying and failing, until eventually she chased one animal to the edge of the water and a drop of her blood fell in. The moment the drop landed, the water around it rumbled and surged. An enormous snake erupted from the watering hole, sending a tidal wave crashing over the shore. This was the Rainbow Snake, a powerful spirit of water who owned all the animals in the area. The sisters hadn't known that, but it didn't matter—the Rainbow Snake opened its jaws and swallowed them and their babies whole.

As the Rainbow Snake prepared to go back to sleep, other snakes arrived, drawn by the commotion. When they asked the Rainbow Snake what had happened, he lied and said it was nothing. But they pressed him, and he finally admitted that he had eaten the two sisters and their kids.

Suddenly a storm arrived. Monsoon winds and rains pelted the Rainbow Snake, forcing him to the ground. His rolling and flailing moved the earth around him, creating a wide river valley. He let out a roar and threw up, spewing the bodies of the sisters and their babies onto the land again, right on top of an anthill. Once the weather cleared, the ants crawled all over the sisters and bit them until, finally, they woke up.

# WHITE BUFFALO CALF WOMAN

## LADY OF THE PLAINS

# WHITE BUFFALO CALF WOMAN

**TRADITION:** American Great Plains/Lakota

**ALSO KNOWN AS:** Ptesanwi (Lakota)

To the native peoples of the Great Plains, the vast grasslands covering the center of North America, no resource was more important than wild buffalo herds. The natives ate buffalo meat, used buffalo skin to make clothes and shelter, and carved buffalo horns and bones to make tools. According to one popular myth, that's all thanks to the White Buffalo Calf Woman.

## THE COMING OF THE WHITE BUFFALO CALF WOMAN

The animals had disappeared, and no one knew where they'd gone. As days turned into weeks and hunters came home empty-handed, the people began to starve. While the elders called a tribal council to debate what to do, two young tribesmen decided to go hunt what they could.

They left before the sun rose and traveled far from camp, listening and squinting through the morning mist. At one point, they thought they saw something moving in the distance. As they crept closer, they saw that it wasn't an animal, but a woman—a beautiful woman, with shining eyes, who moved without her feet touching the ground.

If you ran into a floating stranger in the wilderness, you might be a little scared, and one of the hunters was. But the other hunter wasn't going to let a little supernatural weirdness stop him from flirting with a lady, so he reached out to touch her. In an instant, his whole body erupted in flames, and soon all that was left of him were bones and snakes.

## What's in a Pipe?

You might have heard of the peace pipe—the name European settlers gave to the ceremonial pipes that many Native Americans passed around at the conclusion of a peace treaty. But *peace pipe* is a European term too narrow to describe the actual object.

Many (though not all) Native American tribes used ceremonial pipes for sealing peace treaties, but they also used them for matters of war, trade, diplomacy, and all sorts of rituals and prayers. The look, style, and material of the pipe varies depending on who made it: Some are wood, some are stone, some are long, some are short, and many have feathers or other materials attached. What is smoked inside also varies—usually tobacco, but sometimes other leaves and herbs.

But before you get any ideas, remember that tobacco is addictive, and smoking is very, very bad for your health!

The woman told the other hunter to go home and tell his chief to build a medicine tent with twenty-four poles, and that she would visit later with gifts. The hunter told his chief, the people built the tent, and sure enough, the woman arrived. She told them to set up a red altar and place a buffalo skull and a rack on top. Once that was ready, she circled the tent, opened her bundle, and pulled out a pipe. She showed the people how to hold it—stem with the left hand, bowl with the right—and how to fill it with tobacco and smoke it. She also taught them to pray, sing sacred songs, and walk around the tent in the pattern of the sun.

By the end of the day, she had taught them all the sacred rituals they needed to survive. She stood to leave, promising to return in the next age, and then she walked away. As she headed toward the setting sun, she turned several times, and with each turn she transformed. One turn and she became a white buffalo calf. Two, and she was a black one. After three turns, she was red, and after the fourth she became yellow. And then she was gone.

Soon after, wild buffalo came to live near the people and allowed themselves to be hunted. But the rare white buffalo has been sacred ever since.

# XBALANQUE
# AND HUNAHPU

## THE HERO TWINS

# XBALANQUE AND HUNAHPU

**TRADITION:** Mesoamerican

**HOME:** Primordial earth; later, the sky

Twins have a special significance in Central American mythologies. They are strange and rare and dangerous enough that some nations made a practice of killing one of each pair, just in case. Twin gods created the world and were involved in a number of cataclysmic legends. Twin humans were believed to have a similar, if smaller, power. Good or bad, twins always brought change.

The greatest Mayan myth, the Popol Vuh, tells a story that stretches from creation to the present day—or at least, to the present day of the folks who wrote it. In addition to the actions of gods and monsters, the creation of the universe and the creation of man, it describes the greatest heroes in all of Mayan myth: the Hero Twins, Xbalanque and Hunahpu (pronounced "shi-ball-*lawn*-key" and "hoo-*nah*-poo"). But, it starts with their relatives.

## THE HERO TWINS' LESS HEROIC RELATIVES

The Hero Twins' father and uncle, Hun Hunahpu and Vucub Hunahpu, were twins themselves. They were huge fans of *pitz*, a sacred Mayan game that's sort of like basketball but uses hips instead of hands. They spent most days playing it on their ball court.

The thing was, their court sat right above Xibalba, the underworld, and the gods of the dead could hear every

scuff, squeak, and bounce of the ball on their ceiling. The noise continued day after day after day, until the death gods decided to do something about it.

The gods invited the twins to visit them in Xibalba and arranged traps and tests that they were sure would kill them. They tricked the twins into greeting wooden dummies instead of the gods and burning themselves on scalding-hot furniture. They gave the twins cigars and challenged them to keep them lit for a whole night. And when the twins failed, the gods killed them and chopped them up and threw away the pieces.

> Another example of the odd role of twins in Central American mythology: Xolotl is the Aztec god of deformities and twins.

## THE HERO TWINS

Luckily for us, that wasn't the end of the story. Through a strange series of events, a girl named Xquic had children with Hun Hunahpu's head: another pair of twins named Xbalanque and Hunahpu. These were wild kids. They hunted, played games, turned their mean half brothers into monkeys, and tricked a giant bird monster named Vucub Caquix into letting them replace his eyes with corn. And, like their father and uncle before them, they played pitz in the ball court above Xibalba.

Once again, the death gods got angry, and once again, they sent an invitation to the twins to visit the underworld. But Xbalanque and Hunahpu were tricky guys. Instead of blundering in, they sent a mosquito ahead to scout, with orders to find the death gods, bite them, and then return and warn them about anything it saw while it was down there.

The first things the mosquito bit turned out to be wooden dummies, but then the bug moved on to the actual gods. One by one, the gods all yelled each other's names as they stumbled around trying to swat the mosquito, but it escaped and flew back to Xbalanque and Hunahpu to tell them what it saw.

When the twins arrived in Xibalba, they walked right past the dummies and correctly addressed each death god by name. The death gods offered them a burning seat, but the twins politely refused. The death gods ordered them to keep cigars lit all night, and the twins did so—with fireflies. So the death gods came up with more challenges, forcing them through the House of Knives, the House of Ice, the House of Jaguars, the House of Fire, and even the House of Bats with Knives for Noses.

The challenges just kept coming, until eventually Xbalanque and Hunahpu realized the truth: One way or another, the death gods would keep testing them until they were dead. So, they died.

A week later, they came back to life, disguised themselves as traveling dancers, and offered to dance for the death gods. As they danced, the death gods told them to sacrifice a dog and bring it back to life, so they did. They told them to sacrifice a person and bring them back to life, so they did. They told them to sacrifice themselves and bring themselves back to life, so they did.

By this point the death gods were so excited that they told the twins to sacrifice the head death god and bring him back to life, and the twins did—or, at least, they did the first part. They didn't bring him back to life. They left him dead, and then killed the other death gods, and then rose up into the heavens and became the sun and the moon.

# THE YELLOW EMPEROR

## THE GREAT SOVEREIGN

# THE YELLOW EMPEROR

**TRADITION:** Chinese
**HOME:** The Heavenly Court
**ALSO KNOWN AS:** Huang Di

According to legend, more than four thousand years ago, China was ruled by the Yellow Emperor. He was a gallant leader, a brilliant innovator, and a heroic general who led armies of gods and dragons against the monsters who attacked his people and lands. He fought not to conquer, but to restore and maintain order, so that people could live in peace. Legends also claim he invented wheels, pottery, writing, music, boats, roads, astronomy, and countless agricultural techniques.

There are some who claim the Yellow Emperor might have been an actual person, a tribal leader from China's distant past. Others suggest he might have started out as a god, whom later writers portrayed as a person. It was so long ago that sources are scarce, and it's impossible to say for sure.

## THE WAR FOR CHINA

The Yellow Emperor wasn't the only emperor in his time. He was opposed by another ruler, the Flame Emperor. For a time they managed to rule peacefully, but eventually, the tension between their empires erupted into war. They brought their armies into a battle that would decide, once and for all, who would have dominion over the world. The Flame Emperor fought with fire and drought, but the Yellow Emperor had power over water and rain, which he used to put out the fires and win the war.

NO! MY ONE WEAKNESS!

## CHI YOU'S REBELLION

After his surrender, the Flame Emperor returned to his home to live out his years in peace. The Yellow Emperor, meanwhile, organized a huge parade of friends, allies, and prisoners to celebrate his victory. In the front of the procession rode the emperor himself, in an ivory chariot, pulled by elephants and guarded by dragons, phoenixes, and tigers. In chains and under guard at the back of the procession was one of the Flame Emperor's former generals, the war god Chi You.

Chi You was a proud and powerful god, with a bronze head, iron horns, four eyes, and hooved feet. He hated the Yellow Emperor and dreamed of revenge. Eventually he convinced his guards to aid his escape and sneaked away from the procession.

He headed south to his leader, the Flame Emperor, pledging his service and asking him to pick up the fight again. But the Flame Emperor refused. He was old, tired, and finished with war. He had accepted his loss and wished for peace.

Chi You did not accept peace. He traveled the land, inviting all who hated the Yellow Emperor to join his army. Soon he had thousands of monsters, demons, spirits, and ferocious beasts rallied under his banner, and together they marched back north and readied for battle.

Chi You's army met the Yellow Emperor on an old battlefield scattered with bones and rusted weapons from the last war. But this time, the Yellow Emperor was outmatched. Chi You summoned a magical fog that followed the Yellow Emperor's army, making it impossible for them to see which way they were going. As the army tried to retreat, it found itself surrounded and assaulted on all sides.

The Yellow Emperor's army was hopelessly lost and facing annihilation when he came upon an old man. Seemingly oblivious to the battle raging around him, the old man sat calmly piecing something together. When the Yellow Emperor asked what in the world he was doing, the old man presented the emperor with his invention: the world's first compass. Using the compass, the Yellow Emperor guided his army out of the fog and back into the battle.

After an eternity of war, in which many gods and spirits lost their lives, Chi You was defeated. He was captured and executed, and his army was scattered in all directions. China, at long last, was safe.

# YI

## THE DIVINE ARCHER

## YI

**TRADITION:** Chinese
**HOME:** The sun
**ALSO KNOWN AS:** Hou Yi

"Why did Yi shoot the suns?" asks an ancient book of riddles. Twenty-five hundred years ago, this was a question any Chinese kid could answer. The story was famous: Yi, the god who saved the world, slew gods and monsters, was cursed with mortality, and eventually became the sun (or, in some versions, didn't become the sun and died alone).

## THE GOD WHO KILLED THE SUN(S)

There wasn't always just one sun in the sky. Long, ago, there were ten. The suns were golden crows, children of the Lord of Heaven, Di Jun, and his wife, Xi He, and they lived in a massive tree called Fu Sang that grew in a hot spring far to the east.

Only one sun was allowed in the sky at once. They traded off on a ten-day cycle—first one, then the next, and so on. But they didn't like being stuck on a tree for nine out of every ten days, and one day they all flew into the sky together.

It got warm, and then it got hot, and then it got hotter. Soon the suns' combined heat was turning the world into a scorched desert. Crops failed and people died. The humble ruler of the people of Earth begged Di Jun for help, and Di Jun told his sons to stop being jerks and go back to their tree. But they were having too much fun to listen to his commands.

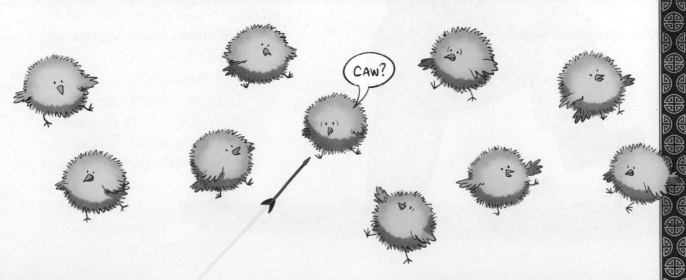

CAW?

You can imagine Di Jun's relief when the divine archer Yi strode in and offered his services. Di Jun sent Yi down to Earth to scare some sense into the suns. But when Yi landed on Earth and saw the death and devastation for himself, he was so enraged that he skipped right past scaring them. He drew his bow, took aim, and fired. There was a burst of sparks and a shower of golden feathers, and one of the suns plummeted to the ground. It was a huge crow, with one of Yi's arrows sticking out of its chest. Yi hardly paused before loosing another arrow, and then another, killing crow after crow until only one sun was left, and the weather finally cooled down.

## THE GOD WHO KILLED SEVERAL OTHER THINGS

BOW TO THE TOOOOOTH!

Some heroes might have stopped after killing a small galaxy's worth of suns, but Yi could see that he was still needed and decided to help the people of Earth.

Horrible storms were blowing across China. Yi tracked their source to the Count of Winds, Fei Lian, and shot him until he stopped. A flooding river was washing away crops, buildings, and people, so Yi shot the river until it stopped. When a river god burst out, surrounded by servants and warriors, Yi shot him until he fled, and then went to shoot one of his servants, but stopped himself when he realized she was a girl. She turned out to be Heng'e, sister of the water god, and she was so grateful that Yi didn't shoot her that she married him.

Yi also shot a one-toothed giant named Chiseltooth; a giant, storm-causing peacock called the Windbird; and, in at least one myth, a dog that ate the moon.

## THE GOD WHO BECAME MORTAL

The people of Earth loved Yi, but Di Jun didn't. Yi, after all, had killed nine of his sons/suns, so Di Jun sentenced Yi and his wife to live on Earth as mortals.

Yi and his wife settled on Earth permanently, but Yi had no intention of dying. He resolved to find the one known antidote to mortality: an elixir owned by a goddess known as the Queen Mother of the West. He journeyed to her home and offered his services in exchange for two servings of the elixir. She named her price, and to Yi's surprise, he didn't have to shoot anybody. He just had to build her a really nice palace.

Yi got to work, and as soon as he was finished, the Queen Mother handed him a vial and a warning: The vial held exactly enough elixir for both him and his wife to become immortal. But if either of them drank both servings, it would take them away from Earth forever.

Elixir in hand, Yi returned home. But before he could share it with his wife, he was called away on more hero work, and this is where the story splits.

In one version, Heng'e learns that drinking both servings will bring her to the moon in a "wonderful" new form. She drinks the whole elixir and winds up trapped on the moon, in the shape of a toad, her only company a rabbit and some old guy who keeps trying (and failing) to cut down a tree. Without the elixir, Yi grows old and dies alone.

In another version, no one warns Heng'e about the vial and she drinks it all out of curiosity. She floats up to the moon but isn't turned into a toad. Yi devotes himself to finding a way to reach her and is eventually restored to godhood as the lord of the palace of the sun. Once every thirty days, he joins Heng'e on the moon, and his light covers it—this is a full moon.

ZEUS

KING OF OLYMPUS

## ZEUS

**TRADITION:** Greek/Roman
**HOME:** Mount Olympus
**ALSO KNOWN AS:** Jupiter (Roman)

In the Western world few gods are better known than Zeus. He is the god of kings and the king of the gods, the greatest power in the Greek pantheon, ruling gods and mortals alike with a muscular arm and a fist full of lightning bolts.

Zeus is a god of storms and order, presiding over oaths and agreements and punishing those who break their word. He also judges disputes between the gods, including several detailed in this book.

But being a god-king doesn't make Zeus a good guy. Despite his high status and important job, most stories about Zeus paint a less-than-regal picture of him. He's irritable and temperamental, tricking friends and hurting people seemingly at random, and while he may be married, Zeus has had enough affairs and children to put him at the center of any Greek god family tree.

To be fair, this isn't entirely Zeus's fault (although a lot of it is). It's partly because of the way Greek and Roman mythology spread. Sometimes, ancient peoples tried to connect their myths to those of their neighbors, for diplomacy or trade or conquest. Sometimes they did this by saying one of their gods was the same as another people's gods—Greece's Zeus becomes Rome's Jupiter, for instance. But almost as often, they claimed that one of their gods had relations with another people's gods. And when the Greeks did this, they usually went with Zeus and claimed that he had "seduced" yet another foreign goddess.

## ZEUS'S TWICE-STOLEN KINGDOM

Zeus wasn't the first king of the gods. That was his granddad, Ouranos, an ancient Mediterranean sky god. Long before any of the Olympian gods were born, Ouranos locked up some of his sons for being big, scary monsters. Their mother, Gaia, didn't like that and got some of their other children, the Titans (including Zeus's father, Kronos), to take Ouranos down. After a brief but literally world-shaking struggle, Kronos got the throne.

Kronos's celebration was cut short, however, when his parents delivered a prophecy: Just like his father, Kronos would someday be overthrown by his own son. His solution was simple and effective. Whenever his wife, Rhea, had a baby, Kronos ate it. Prophecy solved. Of course, Rhea loved her kids and didn't love Kronos eating them. So when she gave birth to her sixth, Zeus, she hid him and tricked Kronos into eating a rock she dressed up to look like a baby.

Zeus grew up in secret, and when he was big and strong, he returned to his father and made him vomit out everyone he had eaten. Then, together with his newly freed brothers and sisters, Zeus fought a ten-year war against Kronos and the rest of the Titans. In the end, the Titans were imprisoned beneath the earth, and Zeus and his siblings ruled the universe.

Zeus and his brothers Poseidon and Hades drew lots to see who would rule what. Hades won the underworld, Poseidon the oceans, and Zeus the air and sky. Our land, the earth, became neutral ground over which they all had dominion.

# INDEX

## ENTRIES BY TYPE

# ENTRIES BY TRADITION

# MYTHOLOGIES

INUIT

NORTHWESTERN
NORTH AMERICAN

AMERICAN
GREAT PLAINS

SOUTHWESTERN
NORTH AMERICAN

HAWAIIAN

MESOAMERICAN

INCAN

MAORI

# AROUND THE WORLD

NORSE

CELTIC

SLAVIC

GREEK/ROMAN

CENTRAL ASIAN

SUMERIAN/
MESOPOTAMIAN/
PERSIAN

EGYPTIAN

WEST
AFRICAN

EAST
AFRICAN

INDIAN/HINDU

CHINESE

JAPANESE/
SHINTO

AUSTRALIAN

# THANKS

to my parents, for keeping me
hardworking and curious, my agent, Kirsten Hall,
for her encouragement, advice, and advocacy, and
all the editors, designers, and marketers at Workman,
including Justin Krasner, Evan Griffith, Amanda Hong,
Colleen AF Venable, Sara Corbett, Phil Conigliaro,
Gordon Whiteside, Selina Meere, Diana Griffin,
and Erin Kibby.

# KORWIN
# BRIGGS

is the creator of *Veritable Hokum*, a webcomic
about weird, funny, fascinating stories from history
and mythology. He lives in New York under
a pile of sketchbooks.